Books by Elmore Leonard

The Bounty Hunters

The Law at Randado

Escape from Five Shadows

Last Stand at Saber River

Hombre

The Big Bounce

The Moonshine War

Valdez Is Coming

Forty Lashes Less One

Mr. Majestyk

Fifty-two Pickup

Swag

Unknown Man No. 89

The Hunted

The Switch

Gunsights

Gold Coast

City Primeval

Split Images

Cat Chaser

Stick

LaBrava

Glitz

Bandits

Touch

Freaky Deaky

Killshot

Get Shorty

Maximum Bob

Rum Punch

Pronto

Riding the Rap

Out of Sight

Cuba Libre

The Tonto Woman and
    Other Western Stories

Be Cool

Pagan Babies

ELMORE LEONARD

THE HUNTED

A Dell Book

A Dell Book
Published by
Dell Publishing
A division of Random House, Inc.
1540 Broadway
New York, New York 10036

Copyright © 1977 by Elmore Leonard

Cover design by Chip Kidd
Cover photo by Bastienne Schmidt

ISBN: 0-440-13425-0

Printed in the United States of America
Published simultaneously in Canada

November 2000
10 9 8 7 6 5 4
OPM

"THERE ARE OTHER WAYS TO GET HOME BEFORE YOUR
TOUR IS UP. YOU CAN GET SHIPPED HOME IN A BODY BAG,
OR YOU CAN PULL A HAT TRICK AND GET THREE
PURPLE HEARTS. IF YOU THINK IT'S WORTH IT."

—In a letter from Michael Cerre, formerly second lieutenant,
1st Recon Battalion, 1st Marine Division;
postmarked December 3, 1970, Da Nang, Vietnam

THE
HUNTED

1

THIS IS THE NEWS story that appeared the next day, in the Sunday edition of the *Detroit Free Press*, page one:

FOUR TOURISTS DIE
IN ISRAELI HOTEL FIRE

TEL AVIV, March 20 (AP)—A predawn fire gutted an eight-story resort hotel Saturday, killing four tourists and injuring 46 others, including guests who leaped from upper-story windows to escape the flames. No Americans were killed, but two were reported injured, including an Ohio woman who jumped from a fourth-floor window.

The blaze swept through the 200-room Park Hotel in Netanya, a Mediterranean resort city about 20 miles north of Tel Aviv.

About 20 Americans escaped from the fire, an American Embassy official said, including a tour group of 17 who arrived in Israel a week ago from Columbus, Ohio.

According to a state radio report, the Park's management had recently considered closing the building after receiving threats from protection racketeers who had failed to extort payments from the hotel's owners.

Firemen extinguished the flames after a seven-hour battle.

IN A SIX-COLUMN picture on the news-photo page of the *Free Press*, several elderly tourists who had escaped the fire were gathered in a group on the street, holding blankets around hunched shoulders. It was raining and they looked wet and cold. A dark, bearded man wearing white trousers, his chest and feet bare, stood apart from the group, somewhat in the background, and seemed to have been moving away when the picture was taken. The bearded man, glancing over his shoulder, was caught in that moment with a startled, open-mouthed expression.

The picture caption repeated most of the facts from the page-one story and quoted Mr. Nathan Fine, leader of the Columbus tour group, as saying, "It's a miracle we're alive. There was somebody went up and down the halls banging on doors, getting people out, telling them to put wet towels over their heads and follow him—crawl along the hall to the outside stairway in back. He must have saved the lives of twenty people. It was lucky, I'll tell you, those stairs were outside, or nobody would be here now."

The man who had gone up and down the halls banging on doors was not identified by name. Outside the hotel that rainy Saturday morning, no one seemed to know who he was or where he had gone.

2

ROSEN FIRST NOTICED the tourist lady on Friday, the day before the fire. He saw her and said to himself, *New York*.

She had the look—a trim forty-year-old who kept herself together: stylish in a quiet way, neatly combed dark hair and sunglasses; tailored beige sundress, about a size eight or ten; expensive cane-trimmed handbag hanging from her shoulder; nothing overdone, no camera case, no tourist lapel badge that said *"Kiss Me, I'm Jewish."* Rosen, watching her walk past the café, liked her thin legs, her high can, and her sensible breasts.

In Netanya the main street came in from the Haifa Road, crossed railroad tracks, and passed through crowded blocks of shops and business places before reaching an open parkway of shrubs and scattered palm trees—Netanya's promenade. Beyond were the beach road and the sea. Looking down on the park were hotels and flat-faced apartment buildings. On the

ground level of these buildings were shops that sold
oriental rugs and jewelry to tourists, and open-air cafés
with striped awnings. One of the cafés, on the north
side of the park, was the Acapulco. There Rosen had
his midmorning coffee with hot milk, and there he was
sitting when he first noticed the trim, New York-
looking tourist lady.

He saw her again that evening at a quarter of ten in
a beige pantsuit and red Arab jewelry, with red ear-
rings dangling below neatly combed dark hair. He
imagined she would smell of bath powder.

She pretended to be interested in looking at
things—at signs, at the bill of fare on the stucco wall of
the café—smiling a little now at the way "Bloody
Mery" was spelled, and "Manhatan" and "te." She
needed something to look at, Rosen decided, because
she was self-conscious, feeling people at the tables
looking at her and making judgments in Hebrew and in
foreign languages. She maintained a pleasant expression, wanting people to like her.

Rosen never worried about what people thought.
Years ago, developing confidence, yes, he'd used to
say, "Fuck 'em." Now he didn't even think about people thinking. He felt good and he looked good, a new
person: face deeply tanned, full beard with streaks of
gray in it. Hair a little thin on top, but the way he
combed it across on a slant, curling over his ears, his
scalp didn't show. He never wore suits anymore. Dark
blue knit shirt open to show the pale blue choker beads
and some chest hair. Contrast was the key. The faded,
washed-out safari jacket with short sleeves and the

fifteen-hundred-dollar gold wristwatch. The outdoor look. The sun-blackened forearms and hands. Authentic casual. Off-white trousers, lined, seventy-five bucks in the U.S., and ten-dollar Israeli sandals. (There were other combinations: fifteen-dollar faded Levi's with two-hundred-dollar Swiss boots; cashmere sportcoat and French jeans. But no business or even leisure suits, no matching outfits.)

He felt that he looked *very* good, in fact, down to one-forty-nine from the hundred and seventy pounds he had carried for more than twenty years. He was also down to five-nine from the five-ten he had measured when he'd gotten out of the service, but that didn't bother him. He still considered himself five-ten and tried to remember not to let his shoulders droop or his gut hang out.

He could hold himself up and in and still sit low, relaxed—the quiet man who knew where he was—a thumb hooked in a tight pants pocket and a pencil-thin Danneman cigar between the fingers of his hand on the metal table. The thumb remained hooked; he would use his cigar hand to raise the demitasse of Turkish coffee.

Rosen was always comfortable in his surroundings. A few days in a new place, like Netanya, and he was at home and would never be taken for a tourist. And after three years in Israel—three years next week—he felt he might even pass for a *Sabra*. Rosen was forty-nine and had been forty-nine for the past year and a half. Sometimes he was younger. For the neat-looking tourist lady, if age came up, he would probably be around forty-six.

He did not change his position, but looked up and gave her the one, "Did you know that if you sit at the Acapulco Café in Netanya long enough everyone you know will pass by? How about a cup of coffee?"

Her smile was natural and she seemed relieved, saved, though she glanced around before sitting down in the chair Rosen offered.

"Are you meeting someone?"

"No, I was just . . . taking a walk." She smiled again, looking toward the open front of the café. "I've been wondering—why do you suppose this place is called the Acapulco? I can't figure it out."

"The owner," Rosen said, "is an immigrant, a Mexican Jew. He came here from Mexico." It was probably true.

"That's interesting. You don't think of Mexico." She hunched over the table, holding her arms. Good rings, a diamond, no wedding band. "I was reading; I think it's eighty-two different nationalities are represented in Israel. People who've come here to live."

"Eighty-three," Rosen said. "The latest figure."

"Really?" She believed him. "Do you, I mean, are you Israeli?"

"I live here. Actually, I live in Jerusalem about eight months—"

"I'm *dying* to see Jerusalem."

"About eight months out of the year. I spend some time up in the Golan, in the mountains. Usually a couple of months in the winter I go down to Eilat."

Carefully, as he spoke, feeling her watching him, Rosen turned the demitasse upside down on the saucer. "It gets too cold in Jerusalem, so I go down to Eilat, the Red Sea area, do some skin-diving around Sharm el Sheikh." The names sounded good, they were coming out easily. "You been to the Sinai?"

"We just got here the day before yesterday. We've been to Tel Aviv, Jaffa—"

"And today was a rest day, uh?"

"Most of the people in the group are a little older. So they set the pace, you might say."

Rosen turned the demitasse cup upright and looked into it, the cup white and fragile in his brown hand. He said, somewhat surprised, "You're with a group?"

"Yes; from Columbus, Ohio. What are you doing?"

"Hadassah ladies?"

"No—"

"United Jewish Appeal."

"No, a group from our temple, B'nai Zion."

"But your husband's not along?"

"What are you doing? Tell me."

"Reading your fortune." He showed her the shapes formed by the wet chocolaty sludge, the residue of the Turkish grounds that had oozed down the insides of the cup while it was inverted. Their heads were close. Rosen caught a hint of perfume with the bath powder. He raised his eyes. Very nice skin, no blemishes. He didn't even see any pores.

"Hmmmm," Rosen said, looking down again. "You're with a group, uh?"

"Why, what do you see?"

"Are you in show business? An actress maybe, or a model?"

"God, no. I work in a medical lab."

"You're a nurse?"

"I used to be, before I was married."

"See that, right there, it looks like a statue? Like Venus, no arms but all the rest. That's you."

"It is?"

"Like you're posing or on a stage, all by yourself."

"I've got two teenaged daughters at home, and I'll tell you, that's not being all by myself."

"But no man around."

"We were divorced."

"How long ago?"

She hesitated. "Three years."

The next question in Rosen's mind—"You fool around?"—remained there. "I see the trip, all those thin lines there, but I don't see you with a group. I see you as sort of a loner."

"If it's your cup," the tourist lady said, looking at him now, "shouldn't it be your fortune?"

Rosen gave her a nice grin. "I didn't think you'd notice that."

"So it's not me who's the loner, it's you. Am I right?"

"Well, in some ways, maybe. But I'm very friendly and easy to get along with." He smiled and offered his brown hand. "Al Rosen."

And the nice-smelling divorced lady on a tour with an elderly group from Columbus, Ohio, was Edie Broder; in Israel for twenty-two days, her first vacation in three years, more interested in the life of the country today than in looking at old stones from Biblical times, though she was dying to see Jerusalem.

And Rosen actually lived there?

Most of the time.

It must be tremendously exciting, *being* here with all that's going on. It must be fascinating.

That's why I've stayed, Rosen said.

It was something she could already feel, the vitality of the people, their *purpose*.

It's something, all right, Rosen said, thinking she should see them getting on a bus in Dizengoff Street.

When you consider all that's been accomplished since just '48. It's fan*tas*tic.

Unbelievable, Rosen said. Maybe she'd have a cocktail?

Edie Broder hoped she didn't sound like a tourist. She couldn't help it. It was what she felt, being here, experiencing it in the light of Judaic history, witnessing the fulfillment of a four-thousand-year-old dream. And on and on for several minutes, Edie Broder from Columbus letting out what she'd been feeling about Israel for the past few days.

Rosen wasn't sure he followed all of it. He nodded, though, paying attention, seeming to enjoy her enthusiasm.

She was kind of sorry now she was stuck with the tour group, when there was *so* much to see.

Rosen followed that all right. He straightened in his chair, waiting.

She would like to see more of how the people *lived*

and learn what they *thought*. Maybe even stay on a kibbutz for a few days, if that was possible. Talk to the *real* people.

"How about a drink?" Rosen said. "Or a glass of wine?"

"Israeli wine?"

"Of course." Rosen raised his cigar to the owner or manager, who was standing inside the café. "The Grenache rosé, Car-mel. Nice and cold, uh?"

The manager came out to them. "Please, you want the rosé wine?"

"Car-mel Avdat," Rosen said, in front of the tourist lady. "Israeli wine."

"Yes please. For two?"

"For two," Rosen said, and he smiled. See? He was patient, very easy to get along with.

Edie Broder leaned toward him on the table again, holding her arms. "Do you speak Hebrew?"

"Oh, a little. Actually, there's only one word you have to know, at least when you're driving. *Meshugah.*"

"Meshugah?"

"That's it. It means 'Idiot.' You yell it at the other drivers," Rosen said and smiled to show he was kidding. "You feel they have spirit, wait till you drive against them."

"Well, I won't have to worry about that," Edie said, almost with a sigh. "I'll be on the big red tour bus."

"I suppose it's comfortable," Rosen said, "but a little slow, uh? I mean a lot of waiting around."

"It takes them forever, the older folks, to get on the bus. But they're dear people and I love them."

"One of them slips and breaks a hip, you've got another delay," Rosen said. He eased lower in the hard chair, getting comfortable. "I think the way to see Israel is in an air-conditioned Mercedes. Start in the north, in the Galilee. There's a little town up there built on a cliff, Sefad, with a great artist colony. And a kibbutz near there, at Sasa. Come down to Tiberias, on the Sea of Galilee. Visit Jericho on the Dead Sea, the oldest city in the world. Hebron, the city of patriarchs, where Abraham's buried. Maybe Ramallah——"

"You make it sound fascinating." Giving him her full attention.

"Spend a week in Jerusalem, then drive through the Negev to the Red Sea, follow the Sinai coast to an oasis on the southernmost tip, Sharm el Sheikh." There, he'd gotten it in again. He paused and looked at her and said quietly, "Why don't you let me be your tour guide?"

She hesitated, knowing he wasn't kidding. "You're serious, aren't you?"

"Uh-huh."

"But you must be busy, have things to do," Edie said, staring back at him.

"Nothing I can't put off." He hoped she wouldn't laugh and say something dumb, like they hardly knew each other.

She didn't. She didn't say anything, in fact, but continued to look at him.

Rosen decided to push on. He said, "I've got an idea. I'm at the Four Seasons. Why don't we take the wine and go sit by the pool, get away from the commercial atmosphere?"

"I'm at the Park," Edie Broder said after a moment. "Why don't we go to my room instead?"

"Well now," Rosen said, straightening.

"I mean we aren't getting any younger," Edie Broder said.

IN ROOM 507 of the Park Hotel, at two-twenty in the morning, Rosen said, "I'll tell you something. Nothing surprises me anymore. You know why? Because I'm never disappointed, no matter what happens."

"You weren't shocked?" A subdued voice coming from the bed. Rosen was over by the bank of dressers in the lamp glow, looking for cigarettes in his superbrief white Jockeys.

"No, I wasn't shocked. Not at all."

"I was," Edie said. "Hearing myself. I've never done that before in my life. But I thought, It's going to happen. I was sure it was because I felt comfortable with you. So I thought, why be coy about it? Like not kissing on the first date."

Rosen was feeling through the pockets of his safari jacket. Passport, sunglasses, a disposable lighter but no cigarettes. "Listen, I thought it was great, except for the last part—'We're not getting any younger.' Don't put yourself down like that."

"I'm facing facts," Edie said.

"Fine, but don't use facts as a putdown. We all have a birthday every year, fine," Rosen said. "I'm forty-five and there's nothing I can do to change it, but so what? Why would I want to?" Rosen paused. "I've got a new theory and I don't know why—it's amazing—I never thought of it before. You want to hear it?"

"Sure."

"You believe in God?"

She took a moment. "I suppose I do."

"This has to do with God's will," Rosen said, "and you either get it right away, what I'm talking about, or you don't."

Edie pushed up on her elbow to look at Rosen in his Jockeys. "Are you a religious person?"

"No, I never was what you'd call religious."

"But you went to temple once in a while, you were Bar Mitzvahed."

"No, as a matter of fact I never was. But listen, living in Jerusalem three years—the Jewish, Christian, and Moslem religions all jammed together there in the Old City—all these holy places, everything directed to the worship of God—maybe some of it rubbed off on me. I started thinking about God and what it might do for me. Then I started thinking about God's will and how people referred to it. Somebody dies, it's God's will. Somebody gets wiped out in business—God's will. You find out you've got cancer or multiple sclerosis—you know what I'm saying?"

"I know," Edie said. "It's supposed to make it easier to accept those things when they happen."

Rosen was ready. "Fine, but nobody says, a person swings a million-dollar deal, it's God's will. It's always something *bad*. So I decided, wait a minute. Why can't the good things that happen to you also be God's will? Like making a couple hundred grand a year tax free."

Yes, and like scoring with stylish ladies who appreciated you and absolutely fucking loved it and knew you weren't going to spread it around or tell the folks back home in Columbus.

"Or like you and I running into each other." He paused, looking toward the open balcony. "Tomorrow evening we'll walk the wall of the Old City, past the Armenian Quarter, and see, across the rooftops, the Dome of the Mosque bathed in moonlight." He turned from the balcony. "No, I wasn't surprised, and not because I had you figured out in any way. But as you said, you knew it was going to happen. I did too, and I accepted it as God's will." Rosen picked up his trousers from the chair and felt the pockets. "I thought I brought some cigarettes."

"I don't know if I can handle that," Edie said, "bringing God into it. I can't say I was thinking about God at the time."

"You don't have to. See, what you do, you aim in the direction you want to go, or to get what you want. But you don't manipulate or force people to do anything. What I mean is, you have to be honest with yourself. You're not out to con anybody; you let things happen and you don't worry about it. That's the key— you don't worry. Something happens or it doesn't."

"What about when something bad happens?" Edie said.

"What's bad? A week later you're telling somebody about it; you're laughing."

"Like if you find out you have terminal cancer."

"Then you're fucked," Rosen said. "No, I'm kidding. There's nothing you can do about that, right? So why fight it? That's the secret. Accept what comes and don't worry about anything you know you can't change."

"It's that simple, huh?" Edie eased back down to the pillow. "Maybe for some people."

"For anybody," Rosen said. "Listen, you didn't know me before. I've learned to be patient. I've almost quit smoking. In fact, it looks like I have. I haven't had a Gelusil in almost a year. And now you and I've met and we're going to have a wonderful time together. . . . You don't smoke, uh?"

"I quit two years ago."

"You don't happen to have a mashed-up pack in the bottom of your purse?" Rosen went into the bathroom and closed the door to take a leak.

It was getting easier to explain his revolutionary Will of God theory. A few months ago it hadn't sounded as clear or foolproof when he'd brought it out in the open. Like the time he'd told the lady at the Jerusalem Hilton about it—in that big, active cocktail lounge—their second day together, and she'd said, "Jesus Christ, I was worried you were a gangster, and you turn out to be a religious freak." He had put down in his mind: *Never talk philosophy with tourist ladies.* Then qualified it later: *At least never talk philosophy with ladies who stay at the Hilton.*

And don't overdo it with any of them. Edie seemed content—why confuse her?—lying in bed with her bare arms and shoulders out of the sheet, watching him as he came from the bathroom into the lamplight again.

"Were you smoking in there?"

"No, I told you, I don't have any." He looked on the low bank of dressers again, catching his reflection in the mirror, the deeply tanned hard body—relatively hard for his age—against the brief white Jockeys.

"I thought I smelled cigarette smoke," Edie said.

"Guess not. . . . Is there any wine left?"

"All gone." Rosen came over and she moved her hip to give him space to sit down. "We can call room service."

"I think it's too late."

"You don't want the waiter to see me. Listen, they've seen everything. You can't shock a room-service waiter."

"I really do think it's too late."

"I can get us a bottle somewhere." He was touching her face, letting his hand slide down to her bare shoulder.

"Isn't everything closed?"

"If you want more wine, I'll get it," Rosen said, though he had no idea where.

"Do we need it?"

Quietly, caressing her: "No, we don't need it." She looked ten years younger in bed, in the lamp glow from across the room. Her breasts were good, hardly any sag—right there under the sheet—and her thighs were firm, with no sign yet of dimples, and not likely to develop any during the next ten days.

Edie sniffed. "I still smell something."

"It's not me," Rosen said. "Must be somebody else."

"No, like smoke. Don't you smell it?"

Rosen sniffed. He got up from the bed and walked across the room sniffing. He stopped. "Yeah—like something burning." He walked through the short hallway to the door, opened it—"Christ!"—and was coughing, choking, as he slammed the door against the smoke billowing in from the fifth-floor hall.

"Christ, the place is on fire!"

He was coughing again, then seeing Edie Broder out of bed naked, seeing her terrified expression as she screamed.

3

TUESDAY, TEN-FORTY A.M.: Rosen was the Acapulco's only customer. He sat with his coffee and pack of cigarettes in the row of tables nearest the street, at the edge of the awning shade. Across the square, above the shrubs and palm trees, the façade of the Goldar Hotel showed its age in the sunlight. Some of the guests from the Park Hotel had been moved there. Others were at the King Solomon. Mr. Fine had taken Edie Broder and the rest of the Columbus group to the Pal Hotel in Tel Aviv, to be near the U.S. Embassy and whatever attaché handled legal matters for American citizens.

It was getting complicated. Why go to Tel Aviv? She could move in with him at the Four Seasons. But Edie felt she should stay with the tour until they decided what they were going to do, and made sure she'd have a flight home if they left, and all that. Rosen said that was the tour leader's responsibility. Edie said yes, except all Mr. Fine talked about was suing the hotel.

She'd be back Tuesday afternoon, promise, ready for
Al Rosen's super five-star Mercedes tour of Israel.

Ordinarily the new Rosen would have accepted this
quietly. If she came back, fine. If she didn't, that was
all right too. But there was a problem. Edie had his
short-sleeved safari jacket, with his passport and pre-
scription sunglasses in the pocket. Up in 507, before
getting the wet towels, he'd jammed his shirt and
jacket into her suitcase, on top of her clothes, and
sailed the suitcase from the balcony, out into the night
and straight down five stories to the pavement. All she
had lost were some bathroom articles and makeup.
He'd lost his sandals.

He should have driven down to Tel Aviv yesterday
and picked up his passport and stuff.

That's where most of the cars were still coming
from—Tel Aviv, sightseers. The cars passed close to
the café, following the circle around the parkway, then
turned off on the beach road north and crept past the
fire-gutted hotel, everybody gawking up at the honey-
comb of empty balconies and at the places where the
cement was singed black. Saturday, the Shabat, had
been the big day, the cars bumper to bumper all around
the square, coming and going.

There were relatively few cars this morning—now
that he thought about it—coming from the street to the
parkway. There were no cars standing along the curb
by the café. It gave Rosen a nice view of the square.

Sunday he had read the account of the fire in the
Jerusalem Post and looked through the Hebrew dailies,
Ma'ariv and *Ha'arez*, for pictures. There had been

photos in all three papers of firemen fighting the blaze, and "before" and "after" shots of the hotel. But no pictures of rescued tourists, or of Rosen walking around without a shirt. So he didn't have to worry about becoming a celebrity.

Still, he was keyed up, experiencing old anxieties, smoking again, into his third pack of cigarettes since Saturday morning. Getting away for a while with Edie felt like a good idea.

He saw the white sedan go past, moving toward the beach. With an Arab driving? It was possible, but not something he was used to seeing. Arabs were usually walking along the road, old men wearing the head scarves, the *kaffiyeh*, and drab, thrown-away clothes, old suitcoats that had never been cleaned. The one in the car wore the traditional *kaffiyeh*—the white with black checkered lines that gave the cloth a grayish look, a doubled black band holding it to his head.

The white car turned left and crept around the circle to the other side of the parkway, the driver maybe looking for something or not knowing where he was going. Rosen could see the front end now on an angle, two vertical ovals on the grille. A BMW. The higher-priced model that would cost roughly thirty thousand in Israel, maybe more. An Arab driving an expensive German automobile around Netanya, an expensive resort town.

Rosen lit a cigarette, keeping an eye on the BMW, waiting for it to come around this end of the circle. When it went past he'd try to get a look at the Arab. He wasn't suspicious, he was curious; he had nothing better to do. He heard the BMW, across the parkway, downshift and pick up speed.

It would probably keep going now and duck into the main street, away from the beach.

But it didn't. The BMW was coming around the near end of the circle. In second gear. Rosen could hear the revs, the engine winding up. He heard the tires begin to screech, the BMW coming through the circle now toward the café, Rosen looking directly at the grille and the broad windshield, thinking that the Arab had better crank it *now*, and knowing in that moment that the dark face under the *kaffiyeh* looking at him through the windshield had no intention of making the curve. Rosen pushed the table as he lunged out of the chair. He saw the owner standing inside the café and the expression on his face, but Rosen did not turn to look around. He was to the walk space between the café and the tables when the BMW jumped the curb and plowed through the first row of tables and kept pushing, taking out part of the second row before the car jerked to a stop and the dark man in the *kaffiyeh* was out, throwing an end of the scarf around the lower part of his face and bringing the heavy Webley military revolver from beneath his coat, aiming it as the owner of the café dropped flat to the tile floor, aiming at Rosen, who was inside now, running toward the back of the place between the counter and a row of tables, and firing the heavy revolver, firing again down the aisle, steadying the outstretched revolver with his left hand and firing quickly now, three times, before

Rosen banged through a doorway and the door slammed closed.

In the ringing silence the man with the Arab scarf across his face stared into the café, making up his mind. He looked down at the owner of the Acapulco on the floor, his face buried in his arms. The man with the Arab scarf turned and looked up the sidewalk in the direction of the shops that sold oriental rugs and jewelry, where the sidewalk passed beneath the arches of a street-front arcade, where people were standing now, watching him. He got into the BMW and backed out, dragging a chair that was hooked to the front bumper, braked hard, and mangled the chair as the BMW shot forward, engine winding, taking the curve into the business street east; and then it was gone.

The owner of the Acapulco got to his hands and knees and looked out toward the street for a moment, then scrambled to his feet and went to the phone behind the counter. No—he remembered the customer—the customer first, and he hurried to the back of the café and opened the door with the sign that said TOILET.

Rosen was standing in the small enclosure, his back to the wall. There was a sound of water, the toilet tank dripping.

"He's gone," the owner of the café said. Rosen stared at him, his eyes strange, and the owner of the café, frightened and bewildered, wasn't sure Rosen understood him. "That man, the Arab, he's gone now." He wanted to say more to Rosen and ask him things, but he could only think of the words in Hebrew.

Finally he said, "Why did he want to do that to you? The Arab. Try to hurt you like that."

"He wasn't an Arab," Rosen said.

The owner of the café tried to speak to Rosen and tried to make him remain while he called the police. But that was all Rosen said before he walked out.

"He wasn't an Arab."

EDIE BRODER, with Rosen's shirt and jacket in her big suitcase and his passport in her tote—anxious, antsy, hardly able to sit still—took a taxi back to Netanya from Tel Aviv and paid one hundred twenty Israeli pounds, almost twenty dollars, for the ride.

It was worth it, arriving at the Four Seasons just a little after one o'clock, in time to have lunch with her new boyfriend, God, as eager as a twenty-year-old but not nearly as cool about it. Her daughters would die. They wouldn't understand a mother having this kind of a feeling. They'd like him, though. He was kind, he was gentle, he was funny. He wasn't nearly as patient as he thought he was. She had to smile, picturing him in his Jockey shorts looking for cigarettes, holding his stomach in and glancing at himself in the mirror. (Telling her he was forty-five when his passport said fifty.) Then very cool with the whole building on fire, knowing exactly what to do, keeping everyone calm as he led them through the smoke. He was great. He might even be perfect. She wouldn't look too far ahead, though, and begin fantasizing about the future. No, as Al Rosen would say, relax and let things happen.

The doorman asked Edie if she was checking in. She told him just to put the bags somewhere, she'd let him know, and went to a house phone to call Rosen's room. There was no answer.

She made a quick run down to the corner of the lobby that looked out on the pool. He wasn't there. He wasn't at the bar, or, looking past the bar, in the dining room.

At the desk she asked if Mr. Rosen had left a message for a Mrs. Broder.

The desk clerk said, "Mr. Rosen——" As he started to turn away, an Israeli woman Edie recognized as a guide with Egged Tours reached the desk and said something in Hebrew. The clerk paused to reply. The tour guide had him now and gave the clerk a barrage of Hebrew, her voice rising, intense. When the clerk turned away again, Edie said, "Mr. Rosen. Did he leave a message——" The clerk walked down to the cashier's counter and came back with something, a sheet of paper, and began talking to the Egged tour guide, who seemed in a rage now and reached the point of almost shouting at the indifferent clerk. The Egged tour woman stopped abruptly and walked away.

"Mr. Rosen," Edie said, trying very hard to remain calm. "I want to know if he left a note for me, Mrs. Broder."

The clerk looked at her vacantly for a moment. "Mr. Rosen? Oh, Mr. Rosen," the clerk said. "He checked out. I believe about an hour ago."

4

MEL BANDY SAID to the good-looking Israeli girl in the jeans and white blouse and no bra, "Actually, the flight was ten minutes early coming into Ben Gurion. So what do they do, they take you off the 707 and pack you on a bus with everybody and you stand out there for fif*teen* minutes to make up for it. How'd you know I was Mr. Bandy?"

"I asked the air hostess," the girl said. "She point you out to me."

"And you're Atalia."

"Yes, or Tali I'm called." She smiled. Nice smile, nice eyes and freckles. "We write to each other sometime, now we meet."

"You got a cute accent," Mel Bandy said. "You're a cute girl," looking down at the open neck of her blouse. Not much there at all, but very tender. Twenty-one years old, out of the Israeli Army, very bright but seemed innocent, spoke Arabic as well as Hebrew and English. She didn't look Jewish.

The guy with her didn't look Jewish either. He looked like an Arab, or Mel Bandy's idea of a young Arab, with the mustache and wild curly hair. The rest of him, the jeans dragging on the ground and the open vinyl jacket, was universal. His name was Mati Harari and he was a Yemenite, supposedly trustworthy. But Mel had seen the guy too many times in Detroit Recorder's Court. White, black, Yemenite, they all looked alike—arraigned on some kind of a hustle.

Mel was carrying an alligator attaché case. He pointed to his red-and-green-trimmed Gucci luggage coming into the terminal on the conveyor loop. The skinny Yemenite picked up the two bags, brushing the porters aside in Hebrew, and Tali smiled and said something to the two Israeli Customs officials, who waved them past. Nothing to it. Mel was surprised. Outside, waiting in front of the terminal while Mati got the car, he said, "I thought it was tight security here."

"They know you are searched before you get here, in New York or Athens." Tali shrugged. "You know— only if they don't like the way you look."

"It's hot here."

"Yes, it's nice, isn't it?"

Mel was sweating in the lightweight gray suit. The next few days he'd take it easy on the booze and all that sour-cream kosher shit he didn't like much anyway, maybe drop about ten pounds. Goddamn shirt, sticking to him—he pulled his silver-gray silk tie down and unbuttoned the collar. Goddamn pants were too tight. He gave Tali his attaché case, took off his suitcoat, and, holding it in front of him, adjusted his crotch. What he'd like to lose was about twenty-five pounds. He hadn't thought it was going to be this hot. Shit, it had been snowing when he'd left Detroit.

The car was a gray Mercedes. Tali wanted Mr. Bandy to get in front so he could see better, but Mel arranged the seating: him and Tali in back. He'd see all he wanted with the girl next to him and also be able to talk to her without the Arab-looking guy listening. He waited, though, until they were out of the airport and passing through open country on the way to Tel Aviv.

"Have you heard from him since we talked on the phone?"

"He didn't call last night or this morning," the girl said. "I don't know where he could be."

Mel Bandy looked over—she sounded genuinely worried—wondering if Rosen was getting into her. Why not? She worked for him. Probably made more than any secretary in Israel. If that's what she was, a secretary.

"You can't call him?"

"I tried three places. He wasn't there."

"He knows when he's supposed to get his money?"

"Yes, of course. Tomorrow, the twenty-sixth of March. Always the twenty-sixth of March and the twenty-sixth of September."

"When'd you last see him?"

"It was . . . a week ago today in Netanya. He wanted to write letters."

"In Netanya. What was he doing there?"

"I don't know. Maybe to swim in the sea."

"Or chasing tail. Was he staying in that hotel?"

"No, another one. I don't know why he was in the hotel that burned," Tali said. She imagined the building on fire, people running out through the smoke. "Did you bring the newspaper with the picture?"

Mel pulled his attaché case from the floor to his lap, opened it, and handed Tali a file folder. "Our hero," Mel said. "See if you recognize him."

She brought the tear sheets out of the folder, glanced at the front-page story, unfolded the sheets, and stared at the photo page, at the figures wrapped in blankets and the bearded, shirtless man in the light-colored trousers.

"Yes, he looks like an Israeli there," Tali said, "but I can see it's Mr. Rosen. We don't have this picture here."

"Wire service," Mel Bandy said. "It was in the *Times*, the *Chicago Tribune*, the Detroit papers, it could've been in every paper in the country—Rosie showing off his body—and he doesn't know it."

"He called you from Netanya?"

"I think that's what he said. But he was—what should I say—upset, distraught? He was shit-scared is what he was. See, I already had my reservation. I told him hang on, call me late Wednesday afternoon at the Pal Hotel, Tel Aviv, we'd work it out together."

"Oh, you were coming here to see him?"

"I told him last month I'd be here sometime in March."

"I didn't know that," the girl said. She had thought Mr. Bandy, Mr. Rosen's lawyer, was here because someone had tried to kill Mr. Rosen. She didn't know of another reason for the lawyer to be here. She didn't want to ask him about it. He looked tired and hot, even in the air-conditioned car.

"It wasn't in the newspapers about a man shooting at anyone," Tali said. "I went to Netanya, but I didn't find out what coffeehouse it was that it happened at. Only that he checked out from the hotel."

Approaching a highway intersection, they followed the curving shortcut lane past a green sign with arrows and the names of towns in Hebrew and English—*Peta Tiqva, Ramla, Tel Aviv*—and past lines of soldiers waiting for rides: girls in mini uniform skirts and young bareheaded men, some of them armed with submachine guns.

"How far is it?" Mel said.

Tali looked at him. "Netanya? I don't think he's there anymore."

"Tel Aviv."

"Oh . . . twenty minutes more."

"How about the money? The guy get it yet?"

"He receive it yesterday," Tali said. "I call when we get to the hotel."

"Have him bring it over as soon as he can."

Tali hesitated, not sure if it was her place to ask questions. "You want to give it to Mr. Rosen yourself?"

"I'm thinking about it," Mel said. "We'll see how it goes."

————

THE BLACK GUY, standing by the open trunk of the BMW, waved in quick come-on gestures to the two Americans walking out of the Ben Gurion terminal building, each carrying a suitcase and a small bag.

The older of the two men, who had the look of a retired professional football player, a line coach, was Gene Valenzuela. His gaze, squinted in the sunglare, moved from the white BMW to the right, to the flow of traffic leaving the airport, and back again to the BMW. Valenzuela had short hair and wore his sport shirt open, the collar tips pointing out to his shoulders, outside his checked sportcoat.

The younger one, Teddy Cass, had long hair he combed with his fingers. He had good shoulders and no hips, the cuffs of his green-and-gold print shirt turned up once. Teddy Cass was saying, "Shit, we could've brought it with us. Anything we want to use."

The black guy was waving at them. "Come on, throw it in. They already took off."

Reaching him, Valenzuela said, "You see their car?"

"Gray Mercedes. Chickie with the nice ass got in with him."

"So they're going the same way we are," Teddy Cass said.

"My man," the black guy said, "any place you are, they four ways to go. They could be going to Jerusalem. They could be going north or south. We got to know it."

In the BMW, driving away from the terminal, Teddy Cass still couldn't get over breezing through Customs without opening a bag.

Gene Valenzuela had the back seat to himself. He had a road map of Israel open on his lap. He would look out the window at the fields and the sun and then look at the map.

The black guy asked, "He see you on the plane?" Leaving it up to either one.

"He was in back with the rabbis and the tour groups," Valenzuela said. "I know what he did, the cheap fuck. The company buys him a first-class ticket and he trades it in on a coach. Makes about a grand. I don't know, maybe he saw us. It doesn't matter. He's gonna see us again."

"We could've brought anything we wanted," Teddy Cass said. "*Any*thing. Shit, I thought it was gonna be so tight I didn't even bring any e-z wider."

"Paper's scarce, but nobody gives a shit. You get all the hash you want," the black guy said. "They say anything to you at Immigration?"

"That's what I'm talking about," Teddy Cass said.

"No, that's Customs. Immigration, the man who looked at your passport." The black guy was holding the BMW at seventy-five, passing cars and tour buses in effortless sweeps. "Man look at mine, he look at me. He look at the passport again. He say, 'Kamal Rashad.' I say, 'That's right.' He say, where was I born? I say, 'It's right there. Dalton, Georgia.' He say, where was my mother and daddy born? I say, 'Dalton, Georgia.' He say, where do I live? I say, 'Detroit, Michigan.' He want to see my ticket, make sure that's where I came from. He say, when was the last time I was in an Arab country? I say I never been to an Arab country. He say,

'But you an Arab.' I say, 'My man, I'm a Muslim. You don't have to be an Arab to be a Muslim.'"

Teddy Cass said, "Kamal Rashad, shit. Clarence Robinson out of Dalton, Detroit, the Wayne County Jail, and Jackson Prison."

"A long way around," Rashad said. "And I ain't goin' back."

"You're not going anywhere, you blow another setup," Valenzuela said.

"Man saw me," Rashad said, looking at the rearview mirror. "He moved. I had five in this big old army piece, that's all. What was I supposed to do? Once I emptied it—see, there was people—I didn't have the time to load and go after him."

"So it doesn't sound like you prepared it," Valenzuela said.

"I didn't have *time*. I had to get a car. I had to buy a gun. I had to locate the man and kill him in like twenty-four hours."

"No you didn't," Valenzuela said. "You had to locate him. That's what I'm saying—you didn't prepare it. You wanted the quick shot and some points. Now the guy's flushed and we gotta find him again. We can assume, I think, he hasn't left the country. Otherwise Mr. Mel Bandy wouldn't be here to see him. That's the only thing we got going for us. But we lose him, you don't get on that Mercedes' ass pretty soon, we might as well go home and wait for another fire."

"We already on it," Rashad said. "Three, four cars ahead of us." Nice. He felt his timing coming back.

Valenzuela leaned forward to lay his arms on the

back of the front seat and study the traffic ahead of them. After a moment he said, "You're gonna have to get another car. Christ, driving around in a white car with red paint all over the front end. Also, we gotta make a contact for guns where we've got a selection, not some rusty shit they picked up in a field."

"I already done it," Rashad said.

"We could've brought our own if somebody'd told us," Teddy Cass said. He was looking out the window as they approached a line of hitchhiking soldiers. He got excited seeing them. "Hey, shit, we could take theirs. You see that?" Teddy Cass twisted in his seat to look back. "What's that they're carrying, M–16s?"

"M–16s and Uzis, the submachine gun," Rashad said. "Fine little weapon. Holds thirty rounds in a banana clip. Fold the stock up on the Uzi, it fit in your briefcase. But you take one off a soldier—I'm told they roadblock the whole fucking country, get your ass in half an hour."

"I like it," Teddy Cass said. "I like the sound. Ouuuzi."

"Five bills on the black," Rashad said. "You want to pay that much. Nice Browning automatic, Beretta Parabellum, we can get for two each. Very popular."

"How about explosives?" Valenzuela said.

"I haven't priced none of that," Rashad said. "I figure that's Teddy's department." He slowed down as he saw the Mercedes, now two cars ahead of them, make a curving right into an intersecting highway. Rashad grinned. "Keeping it easy for us. They going to Tel Aviv."

———

THE FIVE-STAR HOTELS in Tel Aviv are all on the Mediter-ranean on a one-mile stretch of beach: the Dan, the Continental, the Plaza, the Hilton, and the Pal.

Mel Bandy could see the Hilton as they came south on Hayarkon and turned into the Pal. The Hilton looked newer, more modern. The Pal looked put to-gether, its newest wing coming out from the front on pillars, with a parking area and the main entrance be-neath. Tali said oh yes, the Pal was an excellent hotel. Mel Bandy wasn't sure.

He got out of the Mercedes and entered the lobby, pulling at the trousers sticking to his can, and waited while Tali spoke to the desk people in Hebrew, sound-ing like she was arguing with them—good, not taking any shit—then brought out the manager, Mr. Shapira, who was delighted to meet Mr. Bandy from Detroit. Mel was surprised and felt a little better.

Moving to the elevator, he said, "We got a suite?"

Tali looked at the two keys she was holding. "I don't know. I think it's adjoining rooms."

"I told them I wanted a suite."

"Let me ask Mr. Shapira."

"Never mind," Mel said. "Get the bags upstairs and call the guy at the embassy. I'll look at the rooms. I don't like them, we'll have them changed."

Tali said yes, of course. She didn't know if she liked this Mr. Bandy. He wasn't at all like Mr. Rosen.

THE WHITE BMW, motor idling, waited on Hayarkon in front of the Pal.

"Where's the Hilton from here?" Valenzuela was leaning forward again, looking through the windshield.

Rashad pointed. "The one right there. Independence Park in between. You can run it in two minutes."

"Looks better'n this place," Teddy Cass said.

But it was Valenzuela who'd decide. He said, "I don't like to run. I want to be close by, in the same place."

"How do I know where the man's going to stay?" Rashad said. "See, he didn't call me and let me know."

Valenzuela didn't bother to give him a look. He said to Teddy Cass, "Go in, tell them we got a reservation. Two rooms. Wait a minute, tell them you're a friend of Mr. Bandy's. And find out what room he's in."

Teddy Cass got out of the car and walked into the shade of the parking area beneath the new wing.

Valenzuela sat back in the seat, thoughtful. "Where's the gun contact? How far?"

"Cross town, over in the Hatikva Quarter."

"You and Teddy'll go there this afternoon. But you got to watch him. Teddy'll buy the fucking store."

"I'm supposed to meet the man tonight. Ain't somebody you call up and say make it three forty-five instead."

"All right, this evening. How'd you find him?"

"You recall I came here with a name. Friend of a friend."

"Five for an Uzi, huh?"

"Going price yesterday. Subject to change."

"We're not going to worry about that. We're not

gonna go crazy, but we're not gonna skimp either. How about shotguns?"

"I 'magine. Probably buy shotguns on a street corner. This man leans toward the more exotic weapons."

"Teddy wants dynamite or some plastic, C4. He was thinking they got everything here, with all the fucking wars."

"If he's got it in stock," Rashad said. "See, the man's been dealing over the border, in Lebanon, selling everything he can get his hands on."

"We'll make him a better offer," Valenzuela said.

When Teddy Cass came back they saw him nodding before he reached the car.

"Okay, Clarence-Rashad," Valenzuela said. "Check out and come back here. We'll show you how it's done."

5

THE MARINE BEHIND the high counter that was like a judge's bench inside the front entrance of the United States Embassy, Tel Aviv, was Gunnery Sergeant David E. Davis:

Regulation haircut, white cover with the spitshine peak straight over his eyes, blue dress trousers, and short-sleeved tan shirt, the collar open, "Charlie" uniform of the day. He wore four rows of ribbons: all the Vietnam colors, Combat Action Ribbon, Expeditionary Forces Medal, three Unit Citations, two Hearts and a Silver Star. Below the ribbons were an Expert Rifleman badge and the smaller crossed-rifles-on-a-wreath version that indicated "expert with a pistol."

Davis appeared squared away, but with a tarnished look about him: a scrub farmer in his good Sunday shirt and tie. Davis was thirty-four. He had been in the Marines sixteen years. He was getting out of the Corps in exactly twenty-seven days and he couldn't sleep thinking about it. It scared him.

He picked up the phone on the first ring and said, "Sergeant Davis, Post One . . . Oh, how are you? . . . Yeah, I can bring it when I get off duty." There was a hint of a wearing-off southern accent in his voice. "I got to change first and do a few things, so it'll be about an hour and a half. That okay?" He listened to the girl's voice, staring at the round convex mirror above the front entrance. The mirror showed the area behind him all the way to the fenced-off stairway at the end of the lobby. When someone came down the stairs or wanted to go up, the watch-stander on Post One pressed a button and buzzed open the gate in the low metal fence.

He said, "Pal Hotel. What room? . . . Okay, I'll call you from the desk. Listen, I told you I was going on leave? . . . It's like a vacation. I got twenty days coming and I'm taking some before I go home. . . . No, what I'm trying to tell you, I'm going on leave soon as I get off duty. But I'll drop the package off first. . . . Okay, I'll see you in a while."

His gaze lowered from the mirror to the front entrance and the Israeli security guard at his desk next to the glass doors that sealed out the street noises and the sun and the construction dust. The façade of the embassy reminded Davis of a five-story post office, with official U.S. seal, placed by mistake on the street of a Mediterranean city. Inside, the embassy reminded him of a bank—the lobby with the high ceiling, clean, air-conditioned. He was the bank guard. When someone wanted to see the manager he buzzed the gate open. When someone had an appointment upstairs Davis

would call up first before buzzing the person through
the gate. Or he'd direct people to the reading lounge or
to the visa office. Or explain to someone, very politely,
no, you can't stop in and say hi to the ambassador unless you have an appointment. Some of the tourists
came in and were surprised that the ambassador wasn't
there to greet them.

Embassy security guard duty was considered good
duty.

Eight-hour watches, here and at the ambassador's
residence, divided among a complement of seven
Marines under Master Sergeant T. C. Cox of Amarillo,
Texas, twenty-two years in the Corps. Military training two days a week. A hundred hours of language
school, Hebrew. (Davis knew about five words.) Deliver some papers to the consulate in Jerusalem. Pick
somebody up at Ben Gurion. Recommended calisthen-
ics and a three-mile run every morning out at the Marine House in Herzliya Pituah. (Sgt. Willard Mims of
Indianapolis, Indiana, a former 1st Force Recon Marine, ran ten miles every morning, down to Afeka and
back, wearing a flak jacket and combat boots. Davis
would say, "As long as we got Willard, nobody's gonna
fuck with us.") Good quarters. Each man with his own
room in a pair of townhouse condominiums a block
from the sea. Each room comfortable and personal.
(Sgt. Grady Mason from Fort Smith, Arkansas, had
Arab rugs, a brass waterpipe he didn't use, and a Day-
Glo painting on black velvet of the Mosque of Omar.
Stores included refrigerators full of Maccabee beer and
several cases of vodka. Fried eggs, potatoes, bacon,

and pancakes for breakfast. You didn't wear a uniform more than a couple of days a week. Three days off out of every eleven. Good duty.

All the Marines at the Marine House said it was. Davis had asked each of them once, at different times, if they'd ever had bad duty. Each one had thought about it and said no, he'd never had bad duty. Davis had said, What about BLT duty—Battalion Landing Team? No, it was all right; you got to see foreign capitals and get laid. He'd said, What about in Nam? They had all been there and each one of them had thought about it some more and said no, Nam was bad, but it wasn't bad duty, it was part of it. Part of what? Part of being in the Marines.

MSgt. T. C. Cox would look at Davis funny. How could Davis be in the Marines sixteen years and ask questions like that? Davis didn't know. For sixteen years he had been looking for good duty. (He had been to Parris Island, Lejeune, the supply center in Philly, on Med Cruise BLT duty, Gitmo, Barstow, California—Christ—MCB McTureous on Okinawa, and with the 3rd Marines in Vietnam.) Now he was at the end of his fourth tour and still hadn't found any.

Sgt. Mims, roving security guard today, stopped at the Post One desk.

"Top wants to see you before you shove off."

Davis nodded. "Where is he?"

"Down the cafeteria."

He'd see "Top"—MSgt. T. C. Cox—have a cup of coffee with him, and tell him again, "Yeah, I've thought about shipping over, but . . ." Then say, "You want to know the truth? I don't want to stay in, but I don't want to get out either. Do you understand where I'm at? If you do, then explain it to me."

And before he left for good, he'd see about getting somebody to take his place—somebody willing to receive by APO mail every six months a package that contained one hundred thousand dollars in U.S. currency. You could look at it, make sure it was money and not dope or dirty books—there was nothing illegal about receiving money in the mail. Just so you didn't ask too many questions, like, what was the money for? The girl wouldn't tell you anyway. Good-looking girl, too, with a nice little can. He should've gotten to know her better.

A GIRL IN A WHITE bridal gown was having her picture taken in Independence Park, posed in an arbor of shelf rock and shrubbery.

"There's another one," Mel Bandy said. He stood at the bank of windows in the eighth-floor hotel room, looking down at the park. "What is this with the brides?"

"It's very popular for wedding pictures," Tali said, "with the trees and the flowers."

"And the dog walkers. They're having a convention over there, all the dogs, and the owners sitting around on the grass." Mel turned to look at Tali, who was standing between the two beds with the telephone in her hand. "You going to call the manager?"

"I'm thinking the concierge would be the person for something like this."

"I don't care who you call."

She began to dial the number.

"What time's the Marine coming?"

Tali pressed the button down to break the connection. "He said in about an hour and a half."

"You know this guy pretty well, uh?"

"No, I've seen him only sometimes."

"Three years you've been dealing with him, you don't go out together?"

"There was another Marine before him we used. The first one went home. This one, David, I believe it's the third time only he receive it."

"What do you give him?"

"A thousand lira."

"Lira?"

"Israeli pounds."

"That's what, about a hundred and a half?" Mel said. "To hand over a package. The Marine know what it is?"

"Oh yes. Mr. Rosen said, 'Let him look. Show him what it is.' The first one, I believe he thought maybe the money was to buy hashish. I told him no, I wouldn't do something like that, against the law."

"What about the Marine?" Mel said. "What if he gets ideas?"

"No, Mr. Rosen trusts him. He said, 'How is he going to steal it? We know who he is. He works for the embassy.'"

"Does the Marine know who Rosen is?"

"No, I wouldn't tell him that."

"Have they met?"

Tali shook her head. "Mr. Rosen didn't think it was necessary."

"Or a good idea," Mel said. "You going to call the manager?"

"Yes, right now," Tali said. She dialed the concierge, waited, said, "*Shalom,*" and began speaking in Hebrew.

Mel Bandy watched her. "Tell him what you want. You don't have to explain anything."

Tali was listening now and nodding, saying, "*Ken . . . ken,*" then gesturing with her hand as she began speaking again in a stream of Hebrew.

"You don't *ask* him, you *tell* him," Mel said. He came over from the window and took the phone out of her hand.

"This is Mr. Bandy in 824. I want a couple of men up here to move some furniture around. I want a bed moved out and I want a couch brought in . . . a sofa, and a small office refrigerator. . . . No, I said furniture. I want some *furn*iture moved. You understand? One of the beds, the double bed in here, I want it taken out. . . . No, *out*. I want to get rid of it. It takes up too much room. And I want a couch, a sofa, brought in. . . . Jesus Christ," Mel said. He handed the phone to Tali. "Tell them what we want."

LATE AFTERNOON; they were the only ones in the embassy cafeteria: MSgt. Cox stirring two sugars and cream in a fresh cup of coffee; GSgt. Davis with a Heineken, sipping it out of the bottle and trying to explain where he was, which Cox would never understand.

They had already gone through his being nervous, Sgt. Cox saying that if short time scared him, then he had no business stepping down. What was the date of his RELACDU orders? Twenty April. That's all? Shit, Sgt. Cox said, Davis was so short he'd fart and get sand in his face. From today, twenty-seven and a wake-up and he'd be out of the Corps with his DD214. That kind of talk.

Well, Sgt. Cox supposed Davis knew what he was going to do when he got out.

"I don't have any plans, no. But I feel right now it's time. I know, I put in four more years, at least I get some retirement. . . ."

"Some? You get half pay the rest of your life," Sgt. Cox said. "Twelve more years, seventy-five percent for life."

"I know, but if I stay in any longer—this is how I feel—it'll be too late to do anything else."

"Like what?"

"I don't know. But I don't want to be a bank guard. That's the way I feel about it."

"What do you have to be a bank guard for?"

"I mean right now. That's what I feel like."

Sgt. Cox didn't understand that. He squinted at Davis, thinking. "What's your MOS, Administration? You can probably get into I and I."

"Shit no, I've got an oh-three MOS," Davis said. "Oh-three sixty-nine, Infantry Unit Leader."

"I didn't know that." Sgt. Cox paused, giving it more thought. "Well, the way I see it, Davis, you maintain pretty good. Passable service record on MSG duty. Re-up and I'll recommend you to the RSO in Karachi. They'll give you a choice of embassies, depending on openings. I hear Seoul's pretty good duty."

Jesus Christ, Korea. Davis was shaking his head. "No, that's what I'm talking about. Sitting at a guard post, or sitting out at the Marine House shining my shoes, getting ready to sit at the post. You know what I'm saying? What the fuck are we doing here? We're bank guards."

Sgt. Cox was squinting at him again, irritated. "What do we do anywhere? It's what we *do*."

"That's what I'm saying," Davis said.

"You don't like it, then get back into your MOS. You picked it."

"Or get out," Davis said. "See, basically, I'm an infantryman. . . ."

"We all are," Sgt. Cox said. "You're no different."

"Okay, but I'm just speaking for myself, the way I see it. I'm an infantryman without a job. But I wouldn't want the fucking job again if it was to open up. So what am I doing waiting around?"

Sgt. Cox wasn't squinting now, but continued to stare at him. "I think you got a problem, Davis. Finding out where you belong."

Davis almost smiled, relieved. He wanted to, but he didn't. "I probably make it sound more complicated than it is."

"I'll agree with you there," Sgt. Cox said. "We talk

about something, it seems like a fairly simple issue, then you start telling me how you *feel*. What's that got to do with it?"

"Well, I'm gonna go away and think about it." Davis did grin then. "I don't know. I'm liable to come back and ship over again, but I got to be certain what I want to do."

Sgt. Cox hesitated, but decided not to get in any deeper. "You have transportation?"

"I was gonna rent a car, but Raymond Garcia's letting me use his."

"Going hot-rodding, huh? Scare the shit out of the Israelites?"

"No, I'm gonna take it easy," Davis said. "Maybe go down into the Sinai and shoot some birds. Get off by myself and think. I haven't made any real plans."

"Maybe that's your trouble," Sgt. Cox said.

THE PREVIOUS NIGHT in the Hilton bar, Kamal Rashad had been talking to a couple of Canadian U.N. soldiers stationed at Ismailiya on the Canal. Couple of assholes from Guelph, Ontario, sitting at the bar drinking their Maccabees, not knowing shit about anything.

That's what Rashad thought Davis was—walking into the Pal Hotel lobby with his haircut and his canvas bag and carrying a brown-paper package the size of a shoe box—a U.N. soldier.

Going over to the house phones at the end of the desk, Davis passed close to the spot where Rashad was sitting. Rashad saw the USMC and insignia on the olive-green canvas bag. Man had to be something like that with his haircut and suntans: a soldier or a man who worked construction. Rashad was watching the entrance and the pair of elevators that served the new wing of the hotel. He didn't look over at the Marine again until he heard the Marine say to the operator, "Mr. Bandy—can you give me his room number, please? I forgot it."

You never knew, did you? Rashad watched the Marine now. He could've raised his voice a little and said, "Eight two four." He heard the Marine say, "Thank you," and watched him dial the number.

After a moment the Marine said, "It's me. I'm down in the lobby."

Yeah, it's you, Rashad was thinking. But who are you? He waited until the Marine crossed to the elevators, then went to the same house phone and dialed 518.

Teddy Cass answered. Rashad said, "Man look like a soldier boy went up to their room. Had a overnight bag and a package with him." Teddy Cass told him to hang on. When Teddy came back to the phone he said, "Val wants you to stay awake. The guy comes down, follow him. You got it?"

"If I can remember all that," Rashad said.

IT LOOKED LIKE somebody was moving, all the furniture strung along the hall on the eighth floor. The doors of both 823 and 824 were open. Davis stepped aside as two hotel employees came out carrying parts of a bed.

He saw Tali inside 823 and went in when the hallway was clear. She smiled at him as if he were an old friend.

Davis smiled back, handing her the brown-paper package with his name and address on it. "What's going on?"

She gave him a tired little shrug. "I don't know. He wants more room for something."

"Who does?"

"Mr. Bandy. I told you, the lawyer who came from the States. He's in there." She nodded toward the open connecting doors.

Davis could hear him: "You bring the couch? . . . I I said I wanted a *couch*. It goes right there against the wall. . . . Hey, and another chair like this one. And the refrigerator. I'm supposed to have a refrigerator. . . . TALI!"

"He's going to have a heart attack," Davis said.

"I hope so," Tali said.

Mel appeared in the connecting doorway. He was in his socks, his silver-gray tie pulled down, his appearance rumpled, coming apart.

"The hell you doing?"

"Trying to stay out of the way," Tali said. "Mr. Bandy, this is Sergeant Davis."

Mel only glanced at him and nodded, more interested in the package. "That's it, huh?" He came in, taking the package out of Tali's hands, and moved past the double beds to the coffee table by the windows. "Give me a knife or something and get the sergeant a drink. Sarge, what do you like?"

"It doesn't matter. Anything."

Mel was grimacing, pulling at the cord tied around the package. "Tali!"

"I'm here."

"You call room service?"

"They should be here soon. You want something else?"

"Fucking string—see if one of those guys has something to cut it with."

As Tali turned to go, Davis stopped her. He dug a clasp knife from his pants pocket, pried open the blade as he stepped over to where Mel was sitting, and cut the cord from the package.

"Never mind!" Mel called out.

Davis looked at Tali, who gave him the little shrug again. They watched as Mel tore the paper from a light metal box, opened it on his lap, and began taking out packets of U.S. currency, twenty of them, placing them on the coffee table and squaring them off evenly into two stacks.

"You ever see this much money before?" He glanced up at Davis.

"More 'n that," Davis said.

"Where?"

"Parris Island. On payday."

"That doesn't count," Mel said, looking at the currency again. "How much would you say is there?"

"I don't know. The other times, Tali said it was a hundred thousand. But that looks like more."

"How much more?"

"Probably two hundred thousand."

"On the nose," Mel said.

Tali was frowning. "Why is it more this time?"

But Mel was already talking. "Doesn't look like that much, does it? But they're all hundred-dollar bills. You ever wonder about it? Where it goes?"

"Not too much," Davis said. He was wasting time while the guy played with him, showing off. He said to Tali, "Did you want to pay me now? I've got to get going."

"Yes, let me get my purse." Tali went into the adjoining room.

Mel was still watching him. "Where you going?"

"I've got some leave coming," Davis said, "and I'm getting out pretty soon, for good. So I thought I better take it."

"How long you been in?"

"Sixteen years."

"Jesus," Mel said.

"That's about the way I feel," Davis said. He was going to be paid and get out, so he didn't mind talking a little now. The man asked him where he was going, if he'd be staying right around here. Davis said the country wasn't that big. Anywhere you went, you were still around, you might say. Tali came in with her purse and handed him an Israeli thousand-pound note.

"I wanted to mention," Davis said, "I'm borrowing a car from a friend of mine, Sergeant Raymond Garcia. He's the NCO in charge at the consulate in Jerusalem. I've been thinking he'd probably be willing to take over for me, have the package mailed to him. The only thing, he's in Jerusalem. I didn't know if that would make a difference."

He looked from Tali to the heavyset, rumpled guy in the chair, Mr. Bandy, not sure who was going to make the decision. Neither of them said anything.

"He's driving over this evening. I'm supposed to meet him at Norman's. He's got a girlfriend here he'll probably stay with and she'll drive him back." Davis waited.

Tali nodded finally and said, "Yes, I could speak with him."

"Or hold up on it for the time being," Mel said. "Sarge, why don't you let us think about it. What I would like you to do, if it's not too much trouble"— pulling himself, with an effort, out of the chair as he asked the favor—"is stay with Tali while she takes the money downstairs to the hotel safe. Would you do that for us?"

Davis said it wouldn't be any trouble at all. He waited while the guy stacked the money in the metal box, then took it out again and sent Tali to get his attaché case from the next room. He took time to glance at some papers while he emptied the attaché case and threw the papers on the bed. The guy didn't seem very organized. Didn't give a shit at all about other people, Davis decided. A room-service waiter came with a bottle of Scotch and ice while they were still there, but the guy didn't offer a drink now. He'd forgotten about it. He didn't even say anything as they walked out.

IN THE ELEVATOR, Davis waited until the door closed. "What's the matter?"

Tali shook her head. "I don't know. Something is going on. Something strange, but I don't know what it is." She was tense, holding the attaché case at her side.

"And you can't tell me what's wrong."

"I don't see how I can."

"Come to Norman's with me and have a drink."

"I would like to, but I have to go back."

"You work for that guy? Mr. Bandy?"

"In a way I do, I suppose."

"Upstairs, you looked at the money, you said, 'Why is there more this time?' He didn't answer you."

"I don't think he heard me. Or didn't choose to tell me. He doesn't have to."

"What's Mr. Bandy do? Can I ask you that?"

"He's a lawyer."

"In Tel Aviv with two hundred thousand dollars and you don't know why," Davis said, "and you're not sure if you work for him, but you have to get back upstairs."

The elevator door opened. Walking out into the lobby he stopped her, taking her gently by the arm. "Why don't you put the money in the safe and come with me to Norman's? Or don't come with me, but get out of whatever you're in. Okay?"

She shook her head, looking past him, avoiding his eyes. "I can't do that."

"Why?"

"Really, it isn't something to worry about. It isn't even my business to know. You understand? So how can I tell you anything?"

"I'm worried about you," Davis said. "I hardly even know you and I'm worried."

"Don't, please. I'm sorry."

"I'll be at Norman's," Davis said. "If I'm not there later, leave word where you are. Okay?"

He liked the way she was looking at him now. He thought for a moment she might change her mind and come with him. But she said, "Thank you, David," and walked off toward the desk with the attaché case. He watched her, still hearing her voice, realizing it was the first time she had ever said his name.

RASHAD WAS SITTING next to Valenzuela. They had a good view of Davis and the girl. Teddy Cass was across the lobby, looking at a display case containing handmade leather goods.

"Look at him looking at her ass," Rashad said. "He saying, 'I wouldn't mind me some of that.' Man, I wouldn't either."

"That's the briefcase Bandy had on the plane," Valenzuela said. "What'd you say the guy was carrying?"

"Yeah, he doesn't have them now," Rashad said. "Left them upstairs. A brown-paper package and a bag say Marines on it, U-S-M-C. Don't he look like one?"

"He's leaving," Valenzuela said. "Get on him."

Rashad stood up. He waited until Davis was outside before following him. Valenzuela crossed the lobby to where Teddy Cass was looking at himself in the glass case, reflected among the sandals and handbags.

"See anything you like?"

"They're made out of camel hide, all this stuff here."

"No shit," Valenzuela said. "You through, we'll go up and talk to the lawyer."

6

MEL BANDY TOOK his shower in 823. It would be his bedroom. When they got 824 fixed up with a couch and refrigerator, it would be his sitting room, with a single bed in there in case he wanted the girl handy. He didn't like a girl living in the same room with him or using his bathroom.

He had a Scotch with him in the steamy bathroom and sipped it while he dried off and shaved, standing naked in front of the wall mirror. He could use some sun. Drop about twenty-five pounds right out of the middle, where he could grab a handful. He'd always tended to be a little heavy. But at thirty-eight, he told himself, he wasn't in any worse shape than half the guys at the Southfield Athletic Club. Slimmed down, though, or able to hold it in, it made your pecker look longer. He wondered if Rosie was making it with the Israeli girl. He wondered if the Israeli girl was an up-to-date-thinking-today girl about sex. So you didn't have to go through a lot of shit and waste time. Fucking jet lag. He'd get in bed. She'd come in. He'd play it from there. "You must be worn out, all the running around. Why don't you come take a little nappy?"

Mel walked out of the bathroom naked.

Two guys he had never seen before in his life were sitting in the chairs by the windows, each with a drink, the older of the two smoking a cigarette. The younger one, with the hair, grinning.

"Jesus Christ, I think somebody's got the wrong room. Huh? What is this?"

Standing there naked—not at the athletic club, where it was all right—in a hotel room. Wanting to show some poise, but wanting to cover himself.

"No, we got the right room," the older one said. "We've come to visit you."

"You've come to *visit*. You walk right in—I don't even know you." He was looking around for something. The clothes he had taken off were on the floor by his open suitcase.

"You know me," the older guy said. He waited, seeing Mel bending over the suitcase, aiming his white ass at them. "Gene Valenzuela, Mel." It was as though the name goosed him, the way Mel Bandy came up straight and hurried to get into his pants.

"Three years ago . . ." Valenzuela was saying.

Turning, zipping up, Mel began to get himself together and effect a smile.

". . . at the Federal Building in Detroit. I was down there with Harry Manza."

"Sure, I know your name, of course," Mel said. "But I don't believe we ever really met."

"No, as I recall your friend had somebody else representing him with the grand jury," Valenzuela said, "and I guess you handle his business legal work. Is that it?"

The man was being nice, soft-spoken. He knew all about Mel and Mel could feel it. He hoped the man continued to be polite. He hoped the man had a good ear and could sense when someone was telling the truth. He had never imagined himself being alone in an eighth-floor hotel room in this kind of situation. He didn't want to appear nervous. He wanted to calmly get right to the point, show them he wasn't hiding anything. Fortunately, at the moment, he didn't have anything to hide. He didn't have the answer to what they were going to ask him. But they had to realize he was telling the truth.

He didn't know whether to sit down or keep standing. On the dresser there was another room-service glass by the bottle of J&B and the ice. He fixed himself a drink, telling Gene Valenzuela yes, he'd been handling most of the company's legal work for the past several years.

"But the reason you're here," Mel said—after swallowing a good ounce of Scotch and warming up—"you saw the picture in the paper, the fire. If I saw it, I assume you saw it too. So there's no sense in kidding around, is there? You believe I'm in contact with him, since I'm here and I'm his corporate lawyer. But I'll tell you the absolute God's truth, gentlemen—I have no idea where he is."

There. Like making a confession without telling

anything. Mel took his drink over to the bed and sat down on the edge of it.

Valenzuela sipped his Scotch. He said, "You come over to visit the Holy City, Mel? See the Wailing Wall?"

"No-no, I'm here on business. At least I came for business reasons. I'm not gonna try and tell you I'm a tourist. But I haven't heard from him and I haven't been able to contact him. So—I don't know—I'll probably be going back in a couple of days."

"Unless you hear from him."

"That's possible."

"I think you already did," Valenzuela said, "or you wouldn't be here."

"No, I swear I haven't."

"I mean since he almost got run over by a car. What was that? Four days ago."

"Well, yeah, we heard from him at that time. I didn't personally. He called his office."

"And they sent you?"

"Actually I was coming anyway. See if we could locate him and get some papers signed."

"See if you could locate him," Valenzuela said. "Come on, Mel. You didn't have a phone number?"

"Honest to God. Nobody, and I mean *nobody*, knows where he lives."

"What name's he using?"

Mel had known it was coming. He saw no choice but to tell them. As he said, "Rosen," both Valenzuela and the younger guy were looking up, away from him.

Tali came in through the connecting doors. She

stopped and said, "Oh, excuse me," seeing the two visitors and Mr. Bandy sitting on the bed with his shirt off and his hair uncombed. And smiling at her. The first time she had seen him in a good mood since he'd arrived.

"Tali," Mel said, "you want to call room service? Get some more ice and some peanuts and shit, you know, something to nibble on. Use the phone in the other room."

"Not for us," Valenzuela said, looking at the girl. "Tali, you go sit over there by the desk."

She looked at Mel.

"Yeah, if you don't want anything," Mel said, "that's fine."

The desk was built into the row of dressers, at the end nearer the windows. The younger guy reached with his foot to pull the chair out and stared at Tali as she sat down, half-turned from him, to face Mr. Bandy.

Valenzuela said, "What was the name again?"

Mel hesitated. "Rosen."

"Just Rosen?"

"Al Rosen. I think it's Albert."

"It's funny the names they take," Valenzuela said. "Al Rosen. Changes it from Ross to Rosen, like he doesn't want to change it too much and forget who he is. . . . What's he doing now?"

"I really don't have any idea," Mel said. "I haven't been in contact with him at all. In fact, this is the first time the company's asked me to do anything connected with him. I didn't even know where he was."

Tali watched Mr. Bandy, knowing he was lying.

Why? She had no idea who these men were. She jumped as she felt her chair jiggled.

Teddy Cass, his foot still on the rung, said, "How about Tali here? Hey, you ever hear of a man name of Rosen?"

"Do I know him?"

"I asked if you ever heard his name."

She was looking at Mr. Bandy and saw his eyes shift away, offering no help.

"I've heard the name, yes, from Mr. Bandy, but I don't know him."

"Tali's working for me while I'm here," Mel said. "She's called a few hotels asking for a Mr. Rosen. That's about it."

"What I'm wondering," Valenzuela said, "is what he's been living on. He bring some money with him?"

"He must've," Mel said. "Unless he's working."

Valenzuela shook his head. "That doesn't seem likely. There isn't any kind of work over here could support him. I was thinking his company must be sending him money."

"That might be," Mel said.

"But if that's the case," Valenzuela said, "I'd think they'd get tired of carrying him. Three years—what's he done for the company?"

"So maybe they're not carrying him," Mel said.

Valenzuela stared at him for a moment. "For a lawyer you're very agreeable, aren't you?"

Mel shrugged. "Why not? What you say makes sense."

"You look like a pile of white dog shit," Valenzuela

said, "but you're agreeable." He got up out of the chair and walked over to the dresser to put his glass on the room-service tray.

Mel sat with his shoulders drooping, tired. He seemed to shrug. "What can I say? I'm on the wrong side. Guilt by association."

Tali felt the hand of the younger one move over her back as he got up to walk past her. His touch was frightening. The way they stood over Mr. Bandy was frightening. As though they might pick him up and hurt him and he'd do nothing to defend himself. She watched the younger one walk toward the door, hoping he was leaving. But he stooped to pick up a green canvas bag and dropped it on the bed.

Teddy Cass looked at Valenzuela. "Guy comes up with a bag and a package. Leaves without them."

Valenzuela said, "Mel, who's the guy? He work for you?"

"He's a friend of mine," Tali said. "Tell them, please, Mr. Bandy, he's a friend that came to see us. He left, he forgot his bag."

"Jesus Christ," Valenzuela said, "what is this? She winking at you? You keep your fingers crossed it's all right. Where's the package the guy brought?" Valenzuela turned, looking around the room.

"Yes, he brought something for us," Tali said. She got up and went to the dresser, Mr. Bandy and the older man watching her. The younger one was zipping open the canvas bag. "This," Tali said, picking up the J&B.

"He brought you a bottle of booze," Valenzuela said.

Tali nodded. "Yes, as a present for Mr. Bandy coming here. Because I work for him. He was being nice."

"Nothing much in here," Teddy Cass said. "Some dirty clothes." He held up a uniform shirt that had been worn. "Guy's a sergeant in the Marines. What's he doing in Tel Aviv?"

"He works at the embassy," Tali said. "I know him for a little while. We're friends. So he bring us this when my boss comes."

"It was wrapped like a package that'd been mailed," Valenzuela said.

"There was some paper on it." Tali shrugged her shoulders. "I don't know."

"You want the wrapping paper?" Mel said. "I think the room-service guy took it. Gene," he said then. "You mind if I call you Gene? You mind if I suggest you're getting this all out of proportion? You want Ross. Okay. Looking at it from your standpoint I accept that, I understand. But I came here, I planned to come here, *hoping* to see him on business, on the chance of getting a few papers signed. Then this thing happens, he gets his picture in the paper and it's a whole different ball game that I don't know anything about. I think the man's hiding and I don't blame him, do you? He's not a dummy. If he knows people are looking for him he's gonna stay out of sight. Or he might've already left the country. I don't know. Unless I hear from him—which I admit is a possibility—there's no way I can contact him. So the chances are I'm gonna go home with my papers unsigned."

"Well, it sounds like you're giving me some shit," Valenzuela said. "Except you know the position you're in, so I don't think you'd lie to me."

"Listen, I've always been realistic," Mel said. "I'm not gonna hit my head against a wall if I know a situation is beyond my control."

"Or hit it on the pavement down there, eight floors," Valenzuela said. "You hear from him, Mel, give me the papers. I'll get them signed for you."

WHEN MR. BANDY poured another Scotch Tali thought he might get drunk now because he was afraid and didn't know what to do. But he didn't get drunk. He sat in a chair sipping the drink, the cold glass dripping on his stomach, and smoked a cigar. After looking so helpless, almost pathetic, he was composed now and didn't seem worried. She wanted to ask him all the questions that were jumping in her mind.

But they were interrupted. The men came with the furniture and Mr. Bandy went into 824 to tell them where to place the couch and refrigerator and extra chair. When the men left, Mr. Bandy told her what he wanted stocked in the refrigerator: different kinds of cheeses, olives, soda, smoked oysters. She was to make sure there was always ice.

"Mr. Bandy please," Tali said. "Would you tell me what they want?"

"What do you think?" He went over to the couch

and sat very low and relaxed, his head against the cushion, looking up at her.

"I don't *know*. I'm asking you."

"They want to kill him," Mel said. "You understand that much?"

She didn't understand that or anything. Why? Who are they? What is Mr. Rosen, or Mr. Ross? After doing things for him for three years—being paid one thousand pounds a week as his "assistant," as he called her—she realized that she knew nothing about the man. He wasn't a retired American businessman. He was hiding. And these people wanted to kill him. Why?

But Mr. Bandy avoided questions. He said, "You did all right. I liked that about the Scotch being a present. See, they've been watching, we know that now, and they're going to keep watching. So what do we do about it?"

"You told them he might have left Israel," Tali said.

"It's possible. But I don't think he'd go right away, knowing his money was due on the twenty-sixth."

"But why do they want to kill him? Who are they?"

"I'm gonna give him five days. If I don't hear from him by then I'm gonna pack up and go home."

"Why are they watching us?"

"But if he does call, then we're gonna have to be ready with a pretty cute idea. You hungry?"

"What?"

"Call room service and get me . . . I think some roast chicken, baked potato, something they can't fuck up. Bottle of chilled wine. Ask them what kind of pastries they've got. Torte or a Napoleon, you know, something like that."

She didn't understand Mr. Bandy at all. He should be afraid or worried, or at least show some anxiety. But he wasn't worried. He was hungry.

7

THE MAN SEEMED to disappear. He was walking along, up ahead on the wide sidewalk between the buildings and the trees that were spaced along the street, and then he was gone.

It was Dizengoff Street, but ten blocks from the Dizengoff that was the heart of Tel Aviv—a carnival midway of cafés with sidewalk tables, pizza joints, ice-cream stands, and the movie theaters on the Circle. Up at this end, Dizengoff had a few cafés and small stores, but it was quiet and apartment-house residential, without the stream of people on the sidewalk. That's why Rashad couldn't figure out how he'd lost the man. There were only a few other people on the street; it was five-thirty in the afternoon.

He came to about where the man had been: a store-front, a place that looked like it had gone out of business, boarded up and the boards painted red. Except the metal street numbers looked new. 275.

Rashad heard the music before he opened the door.

Something familiar—yeah, Barry Manilow trying to get that feeling. Rashad knew he was going to be surprised. But stepping from a near-empty street into a crowded pub, into a hum of voices and music, also brought him a good feeling, a feeling of pleasure. All the people sitting in booths and at a long row of tables and two deep at the bar—where the guy he'd been following was reaching over a shoulder to take a drink from the barmaid—Rashad liked it right away. A place where everybody was friendly and talked and where the new guy in town could ask dumb questions. A sign over the bar—tacked up over some of the snapshots that were on display and notes that had been pinned there—said HAPPY HOUR—DRINKS 1/2 PRICE. A neighborhood saloon in a city where you could count the no-shit beer-and-whiskey establishments on one hand without using the thumb. But no name outside.

He'd save asking it. He made his way through the Happy Hour crowd toward the bar. Mostly Americans, it looked like. Young dudes in sport shirts or work clothes. American-looking girls, too, dressed for the office, and a few Israeli groupies in tank tops and jeans. There was an English accent, a friendly Limey sound coming from a gutty-looking little guy wearing a hard-hat. He seemed popular, everybody saying things to him. There was a black guy at the corner where the tight little bar made a turn. Rashad kept moving—he didn't need a brother today—finally getting next to the guy he'd been following and saying, "How's a man supposed to get a drink in here?"

Davis glanced at him. "What do you want?"

"Scotch'd be fine."

Davis raised his voice a couple of levels. "Chris, a Scotch here."

The girl behind the bar said, "You changing, Dave?"

"For this gentleman here."

"Oh, right."

Another Limey accent, Rashad thought. Man, a real barmaid, showing her goodies in the blouse as she bent over to pop the tops off some beers.

But talking to the guy named Dave he found out Chris was Australian. The other barmaid, Lillian—who was also very friendly and knew everybody's name—was Israeli. The gutty little guy in the hardhat was Norman, who was from London and owned the place that had no name outside but inside was NOR-MAN'S BAR, THE TAVERN. Dave was Sergeant Dave Davis, on Marine security guard duty at the U.S. Embassy. There were a dart board and a slot machine in the next room, where the cases of Maccabee and Gold Star were stacked up. During Happy Hour there were free hors d'oeuvres and new potatoes baked in their skins. The barmaids also fixed beans and franks and pizza in a closet kitchen off the bar. And in the toilet, after his third Scotch, Rashad stared at an inscription scrawled on the wall that said, "Fuck Kilroy. The co-brahookie's been here." Yes sir, it was a serviceman's-working man's bar. Loud but very friendly.

"Kamal Rashad," Davis said. "Like Kareem Abdul-Jabbar, huh?"

"Yeah, you hear of the famous ones," Rashad said.

"Maybe Elijah Muhammad, the Messenger. But how about Wallace Muhammad? I belong to the Wali Muhammad Mosque Number One in Detroit."

"I guess I don't know anything about the Moslem religion," Davis said. He wasn't sure he wanted to stand here talking about it, either.

"What I believe, mainly, is one thing," Rashad said. "If you take one step toward Allah, he'll take two steps toward you." He sipped his Scotch. "It's a good arrangement and can keep you from fucking up on your way to heaven. How long you say you been in, sixteen years?"

"April twentieth," Davis said.

"And now you don't know whether to stay in or get out."

"I'm getting out," Davis said. "What I don't know is what I'm gonna do."

Rashad tried an approach; see if the redneck United States Marine sipping his glass of Jim Beam would follow along. "I don't imagine you able to put much money aside, being in the service."

"Not at two bucks a drink most places."

"Or have a chance to moonlight at some job, make a little extra."

"I guess I never looked at money as a problem," Davis said.

"Some guys, I understand, they get into deals where they take stuff out of a country with them to make some bread. You understand what I'm saying?"

"What've you got," Davis said, "hash? You want me to put a few kilos in my footlocker?"

"Yeah, I understand they get next to a man going home, pack it in with his personal shit. Man going home from the U.S. Embassy look even better."

"What've you got?" Davis said.

"Excuse me, my man, but have I said I was dealing anything?"

Davis waited, leaning against the bar, the two girls behind him busy, chattering away with customers.

"But say a person did want to ship something," Rashad said. "How would he know if this United States Marine could handle it? Tell if he had the experience or not?"

"He wouldn't. Excuse me a minute, my man," Davis said. He moved off in the direction of the toilet, talking to people on the way.

Rashad fooled around Norman's for seven and a half hours drinking Scotch, trying to get close to the Marine: getting into it again with him—trying to get the Marine to say if he was dealing with somebody or had something going on delivering goods that made him some money—learning one thing interesting, that the Marine was going on a trip tomorrow—but people kept coming up to the Marine or the Marine would see somebody and say excuse me a minute and be gone for a while.

The place was like a club, everybody friendly and knowing one another. Rashad talked to a heavy blonde girl from the British Embassy who undid a couple of buttons on his shirt and moved her hand over his chest while they talked. People would leave, the place would

nearly clear out; then they'd come back and it would
be crowded again.

Norman took off his hardhat and showed him the
nineteen stitches in the crown of his head where he'd
been hit by the drunken Israeli whom he'd asked to
leave and who had come back in with a piece of lumber
from the construction site on the corner. Norman had
the piece of lumber over the bar. He said the Israeli
had sobered up but was still in Assuta Hospital. They
talked about how come Irish people drank and Jews
didn't—except for the guy in Assuta. Scotches kept ap-
pearing in front of Rashad. Chris would say it's on
Norman or it's on Dave or somebody else. Rashad
promised a man he couldn't understand he'd visit him
in Wales, in a town he couldn't pronounce. Rashad
wasn't even sure where Wales was.

The Marine introduced him to another Marine, a
skinny dark-haired sergeant from the U.S. Consulate in
Jerusalem, Raymond something, a Mexican name, and
he watched them standing shoulder to shoulder at the
bar, their Adam's apples going up and down as they
drank their pints of dark. Davis would switch from
whiskey to beer. Listening to him and the Marine from
Jerusalem it sounded like they were arguing, the way
they talked to each other. The Marine from Jerusalem
handed Davis a set of car keys. He said no, he hadn't
brought his shotgun along. Was he supposed to? How
was he supposed to know Davis wanted it? Davis said
because he'd told him. How was he supposed to shoot
any birds without a shotgun? The Marine from
Jerusalem said bullshit he'd told him. He hadn't told

him nothing about a shotgun. Norman came along. He said, "All you want's a shotgun? What else you need? Shells?" Norman had a Krieghoff over-and-under Davis could use, a three-thousand-dollar German beauty you barely had to aim. Norman motioned to Chris to set up a round, took his Campari and soda, and moved off again, adjusting his hardhat.

Rashad got next to Davis again. "You say you going on a trip tomorrow?"

"About ten days."

"Where you going?"

"I don't know. South, I guess."

"What you need the shotgun for?"

"Birds. Do some bird shooting."

And maybe it was for something else he *called* "bird shooting." Maybe he needed a shotgun along for protection. Rashad said, "I wouldn't mind seeing the countryside down there. Whereabouts south?"

But the Marine was bullshitting with the Mexican Marine again. Rashad hit his arm and said, "Hey, you want to go get something to eat?" Davis said they were going to get some Chinese later on.

Rashad lost twenty pounds (three dollars) in the slot machine. He lost a hundred pounds throwing darts to one of the Canadian U.N. soldiers he'd met in the Hilton bar the night before—the asshole slapping him on the back and grinning as if they were a couple of old, old friends.

Rashad sat down in a booth. Young Israeli chicks with long hair would look over at him, the way he was lounging against the wall with one leg up on the bench.

The goddamn guy from Wales he couldn't understand, speaking English as if it were a foreign language, came over with two drinks and started talking to him again while Davis and the Marine from Jerusalem kept yelling at each other and laughing.

A skinny young guy—looked like a street hustler—came in. Israeli, or maybe Arab. Rashad wasn't sure which, but the skinny guy looked familiar. Big high-heeled funny-shoes and a cheap fake-leather jacket. He went over to Davis—everybody went over to him at one time or another—and had a Coca-Cola while he told Davis something, a long story, Davis listening and finally nodding and saying something. One minute laughing, clowning around with the Marine from Jerusalem. The next minute quiet, serious, not showing any of the Jim Beam in him while he listened to the skinny Arab-looking kid. Rashad couldn't remember where he had seen him before. It didn't matter. The skinny kid left and Davis went on drinking.

Rashad closed his eyes. He'd rest a few minutes.

When he opened them Norman was saying to him, "You gonna spend the night here, are you?"

"Where's that Marine?"

"Dave? I don't know. He left."

The place was empty except for Chris and Lillian, and the Welshman hanging on the bar.

Leaving the place, Rashad tried to think of what had been going on just before he'd fallen asleep. The Marine talking to the skinny kid. Yeah. It was cool outside, the street deserted. No taxis, shit, not even any cars. About six blocks to the hotel. He could see the skinny kid—bony face, long hair—drinking his Coca-Cola in the bar. He could see him inside another place then. Yeah, waiting for luggage. The skinny kid and the Israeli girl with the nice ass, meeting the man at the airport. The same girl talking to the Marine in the lobby.

The Marine was gone, but he was still mixed up in it, wasn't he?

8

ROSEN DECIDED there was one employee at the King David who did nothing but watch for him. The guy would say, "Quick, here he comes," and they'd get the basket of fruit up to 732 with the note from Mr. Fink, the manager. "With compliments and sincere good wishes for an enjoyable visit." Rosen had been living in the King David for three years. He'd go to Tel Aviv or Haifa for a couple of days, come back, and find Mr. Fink's note in the fruit.

Usually Rosen ate the banana, apples, and oranges within a couple of days. This time the fruit remained beneath its cellophane wrapper while Rosen paced the floor of his suite and stared out the window. It was a nice view: the lawn and gardens, the cyprus trees around the swimming pool, and, beyond the hotel property, the walls of the Old City at the Jaffa Gate. Directly beneath his window, seven stories down, was the terrace where Paul Newman and Eva Marie Saint had sipped martinis in *Exodus*.

He felt protected within the familiar rooms of his hotel suite. The King David was home; they'd guard his privacy at the desk and the switchboard. But outside, on the road from Netanya to Jerusalem, setting a new personal elapsed-time record of fifty-five minutes, he'd felt vulnerable. The country was too small to hide in for any length of time. He'd have to leave soon, fly to Athens or Paris. But to leave he needed his passport, and to get it he had to find Edie Broder. He pictured her lying in bed looking at him. Yes, at least ten years younger in the dim light. Mature, a grown-up lady, but no excess flesh or fat. Nice tits. He pictured her back home in Columbus, his passport in the pocket of his safari jacket hanging in her closet.

Come on, he had to think.

All right, first try to locate Edie. Check.

Then fly out. Leave the car at Ben Gurion . . .

No, they'd be watching the airport. The colored guy in the *kaffiyeh* would have help by now. Or he might have been replaced. Rosen couldn't get over it: their sending a colored guy to do the job, as if they'd thought it was going to be easy—with only about a hundred and ten colored guys in the whole country—not somebody who'd blend in with the crowd. Christ, they could've gotten a real Arab for twenty bucks.

Instead of Ben Gurion, drive down to Eilat and get an SAS flight to Copenhagen.

No, first call Tali and get the money. Tomorrow was the twenty-sixth. Convert it to pounds on the black market at ten and a half or eleven to one. . . .

Then what? Put it in the bank? What if he didn't

come back to Israel? But how was he going to take it with him? Get a hundred thousand U.S. dollars through the security checks—plus the fifty-something grand he had in a Bank Leumi safe-deposit box? There was too much to think about. Too many loose ends. All right, but arrange to get the money tomorrow or the next day. Call Tali and work something out. Thinking of Tali, he thought of Mel Bandy.

Mel was supposed to be here, when? Today.

Something else to think about. He was coming—they'd said on the phone—to review the business and discuss future plans, which had sounded a little funny to Rosen. They didn't need his approval on anything. Why, after three years out of the business, would they give a shit what he thought about future plans? His business partners seldom contacted him. They sent the money and a Christmas card. Why, all of a sudden, were they sending a lawyer? It hadn't bothered him before, but now it did.

The lawyer arrives the same time a payment is due.

The lawyer arrives the same time somebody is trying to kill me.

Was there a connection?

He was getting off on something else now. He didn't need to imagine problems, he had enough real ones. First, find Edie Broder.

He phoned the Four Seasons in Netanya. There were no messages. He called the Goldar Hotel. The Columbus, Ohio, group had checked out, gone home. The ones at the Pal in Tel Aviv had also checked out. How about Mr. Fine, the tour leader with lawsuits in his eyes? Mr. Fine was at the Samuel. No, he wasn't, the Hotel Samuel said, Mr. Fine had checked out. Voices at the U.S. Embassy knew nothing about a Mr. Fine or the Columbus group.

What Rosen finally did—which would have saved him hours hunched over the phone staring at the wall if he'd thought of it earlier—he called Columbus, Ohio, directory assistance. They didn't have an Edie or an Edith Broder. The closest they could come was E. Broder. Rosen got a teen-aged Broder girl out of bed at four in the morning, eleven o'clock Jerusalem time, and asked for her mother. The sleepy, irritated voice said her mother was in Israel. "Ahhhh," Rosen said. "Where in Israel?" On a tour. "Where on a tour?" With some group. "But the group went home." No, her mother had called; she was with another group. "*What* other group?" The girl couldn't remember. "Think!" Well, it sounded like egghead. "Egged Tours," Rosen said. "Where? Where did she call you from and when?" Tuesday night, from Tel Aviv. "You're a sweet girl," Rosen told her. "I'm going to send you a present." Big deal, the sweet girl said.

Rosen called Egged Tours in Tel Aviv. Yes, a Ms. Edie Broder had joined one of their tours, "Hadassah Holiday," and was staying at the Dan Hotel. Closing in, Rosen called the Dan. The Hadassah group, just a minute . . . had gone to Hadera, to the kibbutz Shemu'el, for the day; returning this evening. Eight hours later: the Hadassah group was back, but Ms. Broder was not in her room. Was there a message? Rosen hesitated, then said yes, ask her to please call Mr. Rosen at the King David, Jerusalem.

He felt better. He felt good enough, in fact, to shower and dress and leave the room for the first time in two days.

Silva, the barman, placed a cocktail napkin in front of him and said, "Mr. Rosen, sir. We haven't been seeing you lately." He poured Scotch over ice, adding a splash of water and a twist. Then put out dishes of nuts and ripe olives.

"Netanya doesn't have it," Rosen said. "There's only one city in Israel."

"Of course, sir." Silva was Portuguese, born in Hong Kong, and spoke with a British-Israeli accent. To Rosen, Silva was the King David. Silva, the oriental carpets, the bellboy who actually rang a bell as he paged and carried the guest's name on a square of blackboard.

Rosen eyed a tourist lady having her lonely cocktail and was tempted. Not bad, though a little too elaborate, with a fixed blonde hairdo you could not muss up, though you might chip it with a hammer. More the Hilton type, lost here in the quiet of the King David's lounge. No, he had enough going on and phone calls to make. Three sundowners and quiet conversation with Silva would do this evening. He dined alone, three tables from the blonde tourist lady, went up to his suite, left it semi-dark, and phoned Tali's apartment.

There was no answer.

He'd been afraid of that. Assuming she had picked Mel up at the airport—this had been arranged more than a week before—she might still be with him, knowing Mel. He'd either be dictating letters, eating, or trying to get into her pants. Rosen wasn't worried about Tali. She was a stand-up little girl. If Mel got obnoxious she'd belt him or else politely walk out. What did worry Rosen was the unknown, what might be going on out there in the near world. Tali was alert, she sensed things, and he wanted to talk to her before he talked to Mel.

Well, he would or he wouldn't. Rosen called the Pal Hotel, asked for Mr. Bandy, and Tali's voice said, "*Ken?*"

"Be cool," Rosen said. "Don't say my name yet. I'm your boyfriend calling or your mother, okay?"

"Where are you?" Her voice low.

"Home. Are you with Mel? Mr. Bandy?"

"He's in the bathroom." Her voice rushed at him then. "There were two men here to see him. They threatened him. I didn't know who they were, the way they were talking, saying things about you, asking questions—"

"It's okay," Rosen said quietly. "Take it easy, okay? What were their names?"

"I don't know. Mr. Bandy said . . . first he was afraid, when they were here and threatened him. Then he wasn't afraid anymore, when they were gone. He was a like a different person. He said . . . a terrible thing."

"What did he say?"

"He said they wanted to kill you." Her voice dropped. "He's coming out."

Rosen could hear the toilet flushing. "Did the money come?"

"Yes, but it was more this time."

He could barely hear her. "What? How much more?"

"Two—"

"Listen, okay, tell him it's me. Tali? Don't worry." He heard her saying, away from the phone, "It's Mr. Rosen."

Rosen sat back in his chair in the semi-dark room, the Jaffa Gate illuminated outside beyond the garden. He looked at his watch. Ten-fifteen. He lit a cigarette and felt ready, a leg up on Mel, ready for Mel's openers. He began to think, If you never liked him much, why did you hire him? . . .

"Rosie, Jesus Christ, man, I been worried sick. I thought you were gonna call this afternoon."

"I didn't know I was supposed to," Rosen said.

"They told you. My flight was due in at one thirty-five. I've been sitting here, Jesus, worried sick."

"How was the flight, Mel? You're feeling a little jet lag, I suppose."

"Rosie—"

"Mel, just a minute. Ross . . . Rosen . . . even Al. But no Rosie, okay?"

"Sorry. Christ, you're worried about that—Gene Valenzuela was here."

"Yeah, go on," Rosen said.

"I mean right *here* in this room. He's looking for you."

"Mel, a guy tries to run over me with a car and takes

five shots at me. You think it's some guy off the street?"

"I mean he walked right in here, he says, 'Where's Ross?' He's not keeping it any secret."

"If *I* already know the guy's after me——" Rosen said. No, forget it. "Mel, tell me what he said."

"He asked me, he wants to know where you are. I told him I had no idea. I said I was here to see you on business, but now I wasn't sure if you'd contact me or not."

"What business?"

"I tried to explain that the reason I was here had nothing to do with what was going on."

"What business, Mel? You said you wanted to see me on business."

"It's not something we can handle over the phone, I mean in any detail," Mel said. "I want to see you—as I told them, it's the reason I'm here—but under the circumstances I think we're gonna have to wait. They'll be watching me like a fucking hawk, every move I make."

"Tomorrow's payday," Rosen said. "I was wondering if it had arrived."

"Yes, the guy brought it, the Marine."

"Did you look, it's all there?"

"Everything's in order." Mel paused. "As a matter of fact there's more this time. Considerably more."

"Why?" Rosen said.

"Jesus Christ, I never heard anybody questioning money coming in."

"Mel, why'm I getting more?"

"I want to sit down and talk to you, Rosie, as I mentioned. But we can't do it over the phone. Right now, the thing to decide is how to get the money to you."

"Why don't you bring it?" Rosen said. "Then we can talk."

"That's exactly what I can't do at the present time," Mel said. "They're on my ass. I go down to the lobby, Valenzeula's sitting there reading the paper."

"What do you want to do, send Tali?"

"Rosie, where are you? You in Tel Aviv?"

"I don't want Tali to deliver it," Rosen said. "You understand? She's not in this."

"Christ, I'm not either," Mel said. "I'm trying to help you on something that doesn't concern me at all, but it's entirely up to you. You tell me where you are or where you're gonna be and I'll get the money to you, somehow, without sending Tali."

"I'll call you back," Rosen said.

"Wait a minute—when?"

"Sometime tomorrow." Rosen hung up.

He lit another cigarette and sat in the evening quiet by the window that faced the Old City. He could still picture in detail the hall in the Detroit Federal Building, could still see Gene Valenzuela and Harry Manza coming along with their attorneys. Valenzuela with his heavy, no-shit look, from the time he had been with the Teamsters and the time he was Harry Manza's construction supervisor: showing the T-shirt beneath the open collar, hair skinned close like a cap over the hard muscle in his head that narrowed his thinking. No style, no imagination. He remembered the time the

Teamsters had walked out and the independent hauler had been trying to talk to Valenzuela, explain things, and Valenzuela listening before beating the shit out of the guy and burning his rig. That was business, his job. The situation now was personal.

All right, how did you get through to somebody like that? Rosen smoked cigarettes and thought about it quietly, trying to keep fear out of it. How did you go about stopping somebody like that?

You didn't; you stayed out of his way. There were no alternatives. Get the money and the passport and run.

9

_____

LEAVING THE BLACK MUSLIM asleep at Norman's hadn't been a bad thing to do. He was a big boy, and if he wanted to drink that much it was up to him.

Waking up with the hangover and the Israeli girl who snored wasn't so bad either. Hangovers were made to be cured with cold beer and hot lamb and peppers stuffed inside pita bread. The girl would still be sleeping when he left. At times, though, he wished he could wake up and remember everything from start to finish. The details came gradually and sometimes, long after, unexpectedly.

He had gone to the Singing Bamboo with Raymond Garcia to meet Raymond's girlfriend Rivka, who was the receptionist at the Australian Embassy. Rivka was depressed. She had fixed up her good friend Sadrin with a date, an American, and the sonofabitch had stood her up. Like it was Davis' or Raymond's fault because the guy was American. Poor Sadrin was sitting home, dressed, alone, playing her piano. Davis said why didn't she go to bed; it was eleven o'clock. Rivka made pouting sounds in Hebrew and Davis said okay, call her.

He went to pick the girl up in Raymond's Z–28, which he'd have for the next two weeks, rumbling along the dark street, feeling the car under him: '72 Z–28 Camaro, the hot setup from here to Jerusalem, a screamer with its 302 V-8, Pirelli radials on American racing mags, lime green with a white stripe that came up over the hood and down the trunk lid to the spoiler.

The next part was weird.

The Israeli girl, Sadrin, wore a yellow dress and pearls and played Chopin on the piano softly. He remembered that. He remembered drinking brandy with lemon and soda. She drank more than he had ever seen an Israeli girl drink as they talked, and she started to laugh at things Davis said. They finished the brandy and got into a bottle of white wine that was starting to turn, the girl laughing and telling him how funny he was. He felt good, he felt attractive to her. She said to him, "You give pleasure to my eyes." She put him in the mood with her crisp yellow dress and pearls—that was one of the strange parts—and her round full lips that he told her looked like a basket of fruit. He didn't know where he'd gotten that, but she liked it and laughed some more and when they started kissing it felt like she was sucking his mouth, trying to get him all in. It was good, but it was hard work and she wore him out in bed, working away, her mouth clamped to his, Davis thinking she was never going to come, thinking what the fuck am I doing here? But he saw her

in her yellow dress and pearls sitting alone. He remembered how glad she had been to see him, to see somebody, anybody, and he let her work at it as long as she
wanted, finally getting his mouth free and telling her
she was pretty—she wasn't bad—and that he loved her
mouth and her eyes and her body—much bigger and
heavier out of the yellow dress—telling her nice things
as he held on and she bucked against him. She went
into the bathroom after and got sick in the washbasin.
She moaned and told him she didn't feel good and
wanted to die and didn't have an aspirin. She went to
sleep, that big girl, calling for her mother in Hebrew.

Out at the Marine House—he didn't see anyone
around—Davis got cleaned up: put on a shirt and jeans
and a white snap-peak civilian cap he liked that was
broken in, well shaped. He liked to wear it low over his
eyes when he was hung over . . . taking time now to eat
a couple of egg-and-onion sandwiches with two ice-
cold Maccabees. Jesus, he was reborn.

He threw extra clothes into a valpac and gathered
up a pile of *Louisville Courier-Journal*s his aunt had sent
him. What else? Stop by Norman's apartment in
Ramat Aviv for the shotgun. What else? See Tali and
pick up his travel bag full of dirty clothes. Something
else. Shit yes, first he was supposed to meet her friend,
Mati Harari. At eleven o'clock.

It was twenty to eleven when he drove away from
the Marine House and passed gungy Willard Mims
jogging back from Afeka in his flak jacket and combat
boots. A beer with Norman, in his underwear, took a
few minutes. Still, it was only eleven-fifteen when he

pulled up in front of the M&A Club on Hayarkon, half a block from the Pal.

He remembered something else he hadn't thought of in the past twelve hours or more and it gave him a sinking feeling. Twenty-six days to go and he'd be on his own.

THE M&A—Miguel and Ali's, where Argentina met the Middle East—was a place with a courtyard in front, hidden from the street; it had white stucco walls with dark beams, and impressionist paintings. Not a drinking bar like Norman's, a conversation bar where young Israelis who were making it came in to talk and play backgammon and sip coffee or one glass of wine for an hour. Each time Davis came to the M&A he liked it, the atmosphere, and promised himself to come back and learn how to play backgammon. But he usually ended up at Norman's.

He asked Mati if he wanted something to drink. Mati shook his head. There was no one in the place except Mati Harari, Tali's friend, and Miguel's wife, Orah, behind the small bar. Davis got himself an ice-cold Gold Star from her before he sat down with Mati and saw his Marine travel bag on the bench.

"You brought it. Good."

"Man, she's anxious to see you. But you got to not go in through the front."

"I've got to not go in through the front, uh?"

"I'm suppose to show you a way, how you take the lift from the lower level."

"What're you nervous for?"

"You talking about? I'm not nervous. Listen, they watching them, man. Tali don't know what's going on."

"I don't either," Davis said. "I don't even know what you're telling me."

"I'm not going to tell you nothing, so don't ask me." Like, try and make me. The street kid, the dark Sephardim with his bandit mustache and his bushy Israeli 'fro. He could look mean, all right, and Tali had said he'd served time in Haifa. Davis accepted that. The guy was still about a Grade C hotshot. He'd last about two minutes on the line.

"I don't think we're getting anywhere," Davis said. "Is there anything else?"

"Follow me," Mati said. "That's all you got to do."

RASHAD WAS ACROSS the street from the Pal at Kopel "Drive Your Self" Ltd., seeing the man about getting a Mercedes before he dumped the BMW. Rashad wasn't watching for anything. He had moved away from the counter and was standing in the open doorway while the Kopel agent shuffled through his papers. Rashad was in the right place to see them coming along Hayarkon, walking in the street. When the Kopel man said, "Here it is," and began to quote rates, Rashad turned to him and said, "Hold it, my man. Before we get into that, let me use your phone. Got to call my father."

Valenzuela answered. Rashad said, "He's back,

coming down the street this way . . . the Marine, man. I'm across the street at the car rental. The Marine's with the Arab kid again. Same one as last night . . . Wait a minute. No, they're going down the side street next to the hotel. The Marine's got his overnight bag again . . . going down there like they heading for the beach. . . . I don't know, maybe he's got something going with the cute Arab kid." Rashad listened, nodding—"Yeah, all right"—and he hung up.

He said to the Kopel agent, "Sorry. My father say I got to come right home."

THROUGH A GRAY BASEMENT hallway and up a service elevator to eight. Tali was waiting for them, the door to 824 open.

"You're very good to come, David. I hope this isn't bothering your trip."

"No bother," Davis said. Entering, he picked up his travel bag from the bed. "I thought you just wanted to give me my dirty laundry."

"Mr. Bandy would like to speak to you," Tali said. "Sit down, please."

The room was like a living room now. Davis glanced around as he walked over to the windows. Now wait for the important lawyer. He looked out at Tel Aviv, at the scattering of highrises that rose out of the tan five-story skyline, the eastern Mediterranean going to glass walls. Somebody had said to him, "Tel Aviv used to be an ugly town. Now they're building all these Hiltons and Sheratons to hide the view of the sea and it's uglier than it was before." Davis liked Tel Aviv. He wasn't sure why. He liked the people, the younger ones. He'd like to get to know some of their troopers, talk to them. He wouldn't have minded having some of them along in Vietnam. Shit yes, pros; hard fuckers.

"There he is. How you doing, Sergeant? What can I get you?"

Davis turned to see Mel Bandy coming through the connecting doors. He looked different, his face pink, flushed—the guy coming all the way over to shake hands this time, trying to give Davis a good firm one with his fat hand, smelling good of something, all slicked up in a light blue outfit—light blue print shirt with a movie-star collar, light blue slacks, white belt, white loafers with little gold chains on them.

"We're set up, finally," Mel said. "What would you like?"

"Beer'd be fine," Davis said.

"Shit. You name the one thing—Tali, call room service. Get the sergeant some beer."

"No, I don't care. Anything'll be fine."

Mel went to the bar that was set up on the desk and began fooling with bottles, bending over, showing his big can as he got ice and mix from the refrigerator wedged into the desk opening.

"Where you from, Sergeant? I detect an accent."

Davis said, well, he'd been born in Harlan County, Kentucky, but had moved from there when he was six years old. His dad had been killed in a coal-mine accident. They'd moved—he and his mom and sister—they'd gone to live with his aunt, who had a farm in Shelby County. That was about halfway between Lexington and Louisville—Tali and the street kid, Mati, watching him, not having any idea what he was talking about. He'd gone to school one year in Cincinnati, but it was in Louisville that he'd enlisted in the Marines. Boring, Christ, hearing himself. He felt like a straight man when Mel came over and handed him a frosty drink.

"Hundred-proof pure Kentucky bourbon. How about that."

Like it was a treat and all Davis drank was some kind of piss-poor shine. The guy wanted to do more than talk. He wanted something. The drink was all right, something like a bourbon collins. The guy didn't offer Tali or the street kid a drink. He made a Scotch for himself and sank down on the couch with one short leg stretched out. He wore light blue socks, too. Davis sat in a chair by the windows. He wasn't in a hurry, but if the guy farted around too long he'd tell him he was. Eleven-thirty Friday morning sitting around having a two-man party. Tali sat quietly, a little expectantly; the street kid hunched over in a straight chair, his dark-skinned left hand holding his right fist.

Davis looked over at Mati. He said, "Don't you want something to drink?"

"No . . . nothing." Straightening awkwardly, shaking his head.

Okay, he had tried. Davis looked at the light blue lawyer. "Are we waiting for something?"

"As a matter of fact, we're waiting for a phone

call," Mel said. "But I want to take a little time, fill you in first."

The guy was ahead of him, assuming things.

"I'm on leave," Davis said.

"So you got time. Good."

It wasn't what he'd meant. "My car's packed. I'm ready to go." Shit, it still didn't sound right. "I mean I've made plans," Davis said. "I'm taking a trip."

"I understand that," Mel said. "All I want you to do is drop something off for me."

"Where?"

"That's what we're waiting to find out. How's your drink?"

"I'll have another one."

Mel pushed himself up and went over to the bar with their glasses.

"You recall the package, the money. You give it to Tali, right? She's the one set it up, she delivers it. That's the way it's been. This time I want *you* to deliver it. You saw it yesterday? Two hundred grand? *That* money." Mixing drinks, Mel spoke with his back to Davis. "We get a phone call from an individual, a client of mine. He tells us where to make the delivery. You go there and give him the money. He calls again, tells me he's got it. That's all you have to do."

Mel opened the desk drawer and took out a packet of bills. He walked over to Davis and dropped the packet in his lap as he handed him a fresh frosty bourbon.

"A thousand U.S. bucks. That look about right?"

Davis picked it up, fingering the packet of crisp

hundred-dollar bills. He watched Mel get his Scotch and shuffle back to the couch, the big dealer.

"If it's such a pissy little job, how come a thousand?" Davis said.

"Looking for the catch, uh?" Mel grinned at him. "Well, I'm not gonna lie to you. There could be—there's a very slight chance of a complication. But not if we do it right. Okay, you want the whole story?"

"I wouldn't mind knowing a little bit more," Davis said.

"I'm not gonna give you details, it's a long story," Mel said, "*but*. There's a man by the name of Al Rosen living here who used to live in Detroit. Three years ago he testified for the Justice Department before a federal grand jury. The Justice Department wanted to indict two individuals for murder and they persuaded my client, Mr. Rosen, against my advisement, to testify as a key witness. Okay, the two individuals were never brought to trial and my client was left standing there in his underwear. You follow me?"

"You say his name's Al Rosen?" Davis said.

"Right, Albert Rosen," Mel said. "One of the individuals he testified against had a stroke. He's still alive but he's fucked up, paralyzed on one side, doesn't talk right. The other one served nine months in Lewisburg on a separate, minor indictment—conspiring to defraud. One day my client's car blows up, killing a gas station attendant who had come on a service call. It was a cold morning, the car wouldn't start. Otherwise it would've been my client. You understand? So my client, with the help—if you want to call it help—of the Justice Department, which got him into this, changed his identity and came here to live."

"Who sends the money?" Davis said.

"That's another story. Well, let's just say the company he used to be with," Mel said. "In the mortgage loan business. The company's been carrying him the past three years and we're the only ones who know where he is. Everything's fine . . . relatively. So what happens? Rosen gets his picture in the paper."

"Here?"

"No, it wasn't even in the papers here. The story was about the hotel that burned down last week in Netanya. No, Rosen shows up in the Detroit papers and some others, picture of him standing out in front of the hotel."

Davis was nodding.

"You got it now?" Mel said. "Three days later, not wasting any time, somebody makes an attempt on his life. Yesterday two guys came to see me. They want to know where he is. If I'm here in Tel Aviv then it must be to see Rosen. So they're watching me. They're watching Tali. They're watching the kid here, maybe. Rosen wants to get the hell out and hide someplace else. Change his identity again. But he has to pick up his money first, and we can't deliver it because these guys are watching. They know who we are."

"Okay," Davis said.

"Just like that?" Mel seemed a little surprised. "Great."

"You haven't told him," Tali said. "They also know who David is."

"No, they don't know him," Mel said. "Maybe they saw him talking to you in the lobby."

"It's the same thing," Tali said.

Mel was staring at her, giving her a look. "They don't know his name or what he does, where he lives. That's quite a difference." He turned to look at Davis. "Of course it's up to you, Sergeant. If you'd just as soon pass up a quick thou."

"I'll do it," Davis said. "Where's the money?"

Mel gave him his grin. "You're not getting any ideas, are you, Sergeant?"

Davis didn't say anything. He grinned back.

HE LISTENED to the plan Mel described. There wasn't much to it.

They had the metal box that the money had been mailed in wrapped up again with paper and string.

When Rosen called, Mati Harari would take the package, walk through the lobby, get in the Mercedes, and drive off.

A few minutes later, Davis, with the money in Mel's briefcase and the briefcase in Davis' travel bag, would leave by the service entrance. He'd cut through the beach parking area next to the hotel and come out on Hayarkon, where his car was parked in front of the M&A Club. Some plan.

If anyone tried to stop him—well, Davis was not expected to resist. "Unless you want to," Mel said, and then asked him if he'd been in Vietnam. Davis nodded. Mel said, "Well, as I say, it's up to you, considering the remote possibility anything happens. But I can't imagine a Marine taking any shit from anybody."

Davis said, "It's about all a Marine takes."

They sat around waiting. Mel would go into the adjoining room for a while and come out looking at his watch, showing Davis he was as anxious as anybody. He'd walk around with his hands in his pockets, his shoulders hunched. Once he went over to the window and looked down at Independence Park, where the brides had their pictures taken and people walked their dogs, and said he bet fags hung out down there, it looked like a fag park. He didn't offer any more frosty drinks.

At about one-thirty Mel decided it was time to eat and asked Davis what he wanted. Davis said, I guess *shwarma*. Mel said, What the fuck's *shwarma?* And Davis told him—lamb and stuff inside pita. Mel told Tali he'd have a cheese and mushroom omelette and fries. He didn't ask Mati what he wanted. Tali did, and then got on the phone to room service and began speaking Hebrew.

After a few moments she placed her hand over the speaker and said to Mel, "They can't put the dairy and meat dishes on the same table."

"What dairy dishes?"

"The omelette."

"Tell them eggs are from chickens, for Christ sake."

"The cheese in it," Tali said.

"Jesus Christ," Mel said to Davis. "You believe it? Then tell them to put it on two tables," he said to Tali. "I don't give a shit how many tables they use."

That was as interesting as it got, sitting around waiting. Davis talked to Tali a little, asking her about her year in the Israeli Army, and found out where she lived. But he couldn't relax and say funny things to her with Mel in the room.

Finally, going on four, the phone rang and Tali answered it. He knew it was Rosen from the way she turned and looked at him before she looked at Mr. Bandy and held out the phone, nodding.

Davis didn't hear much from where he was sitting. Mel stood with one hand in his pocket looking up at the wall, saying, "Yes . . . of course . . . we've been waiting, we're ready to go," his tone much different, being efficient and a little kissy-ass. He waved the phone at Tali and said, "Here, you get the directions from him. Make sure it's clear." Then he said into the phone, "Rosie, don't worry about a thing. It's as good as done."

Tali spoke to him again. When she hung up she seemed sad. "The address where he is is Rehov Bilu 30 in Herzliya."

"I know about where it is," Davis said.

"Write it down for him," Mel said. "What is it, a house, what?"

"An apartment. Number 23 on the fifth floor. It belongs to a friend of his," Tali said. "There's a lift you take."

Mati picked up the package and left, not looking back when Tali said something to him in Hebrew.

A few minutes later it was Davis' turn, carrying the alligator attaché case inside the Marine travel bag and the thousand bucks in his back pocket. At the door, Tali said, "If you come back this way on your trip, please stop and tell me how Mr. Rosen is, how he looks."

Davis left, wondering if Tali was sleeping with the guy. He was anxious to see this Mr. Rosen.

MATI GOT no more than three strides out of the elevator before Teddy Cass hit him with a stand-up body block, forearms into Mati's chest, and pushed him back inside. Valenzuela came in after them. The doors closed and the elevator went up. Teddy Cass held Mati against the wall, his forearm now against the skinny kid's throat, staring at the kid's wide-open eyes while Valenzuela ripped open the package.

"Bullshit time," Valenzuela said. "Paper in a tin box." The elevator stopped. Valenzuela jabbed the button for the lobby. "We'll bring him along."

Rashad was over by the taxi stand to the left of the hotel entrance, where a cement stairway led down to the side street that sloped toward the beach. Rashad waited for them as they came out with the Arab-looking kid between them, the kid looking very frightened or sick.

"The decoy," Teddy Cass said.

"Car down the street's got a Marine thing on the windshield. They like to tell you what they do, don't they?" Rashad said. Next to him, on the cement wall at the top of the stairway, was a plaid overnight bag. "Looks like he should be along any time now. It's one way, so he's got to come toward the hotel before he turns to go anyplace else." Rashad picked up the overnight bag. "I'll see you gentlemen."

He walked down the hotel drive toward Hayarkon and gave a little wave without looking back.

Valenzuela and Teddy Cass walked Mati over to the white BMW parked in the shade of the hotel.

10

HE'D GO WEST on Nordau to Ibn Gvirol, then cut over to the Haifa Road. He could keep going north after the stop in Herzliya, drive up to the Golan or Metulla, see if maybe there was some action along the border—terrorists sneaking in. Maybe talk to the troops up there on border watch. He could still make the Sinai in a day.

Davis put the Camaro in gear and got almost to the end of the block. The crazy Black Muslim came running out into the street right in front of him, grinning and holding up his hand. Davis recognized him, couldn't miss him, as he braked to a stop. Next thing, the guy had the door open and was getting in.

"What way we going?"

Davis pushed the gear into neutral. He didn't like it, but he didn't have time to think.

"I'm going north."

"That's fine with me," Rashad said. "I'm ready to see some country." Davis didn't move and Rashad eased up a little. "I don't want to fuck up your plans, my man. You don't want me along, say it. But I would appreciate a lift out of Tel Aviv. Place is beginning to press down on me. . . ."

Davis started up, creeping, and made the turn at Nordau.

". . . All the nightlife, places like Norman's. Man, it's warm and friendly, but it gets to you. Hey, I thought we were gonna have some Chinese."

That was the way it went. Rashad talking, Davis holding on to the steering wheel. Rashad admiring the gutty sound of the Z–28, saying shit, this machine ought to blow the mothers off the road, put a Mercedes on the trailer. Davis began to relax. An insistent Israeli car horn would sound behind them at a light and Davis would give it some revs with the clutch in, letting the horn-blower have some heavy varooms, then release the clutch and sling-shoot the Camaro away from the light. Kid stuff, with gas a buck sixty a gallon. But he enjoyed it once in a while and the black guy ate it up. The guy didn't seem so bad when he wasn't trying to come on, when he relaxed. He asked Davis was that all he had, the one bag? It was on the back seat. Davis said no, he had stuff in the trunk. Some newspapers his aunt had sent him. Rashad said he liked to travel light. He unzipped his plaid bag and pulled out a white and black *kaffiyeh* and draped it over his natural, saying, man, it made sense. It was cool, and he meant *cool* cool. The guy tried to be entertaining, trying to be friendly. He was tiresome.

On the highway, the Haifa Road, Davis said, "I got to make a stop in Herzliya. It's a suburb up here."

"You going to be long?" Rashad laughed then, taking off the *kaffiyeh*. "Shit, like it makes any difference. Man, I don't even know where I'm going. But if you want me to get out up here, say it. It won't hurt my feelings any. You've been very kind and I appreciate it. I suppose after talking to you last night and all, meeting your friends," Rashad said, "I feel like I'm one of them."

"Well, I don't think I'll be too long," Davis said. Dumb. Backing down because he felt sorry for the guy. He didn't say anything else until they were in Herzliya, passing streets lined with new apartment buildings.

"I'm looking for Bilu. That's the name of the street."

"You never been here before?"

"Well, it's not a friend," Davis said. "I just have to stop and see a guy for a minute."

ROSEN HEARD the car, the rumbling engine sound. He stepped out onto the balcony to see it roll into the blacktop parking area facing the building: a lime-green American car among the European minis. That would be the Marine.

Except there were two people in the car. Rosen watched the driver, in a white cap, get out and reach in again to get the canvas bag, then slam the door and start toward the building.

Rosen stepped back, a reflex action. He could still see the car and make out the figure sitting in the front seat. He didn't see the man's face, though, until the side window came down and the face inside leaned over to look up at the building. Rosen jumped back again.

The guy in the car was black.

He told himself it couldn't be the same one. Probably another Marine or a guy who worked at the embassy. When he heard the elevator coming up—one door away in the hall—he stepped out to the balcony again. The black guy was still in the car. If it was the one from Netanya he wouldn't be sitting there doing nothing. Rosen went to the door of the apartment and opened it about an inch, then moved to a table facing the door where his attaché case was lying open, the top half of it standing up. The small automatic pistol he brought out of the attaché case was wrapped in tissue paper.

He didn't know for sure that the guy in the cap was the Marine named Davis. Or if the guy was coming here. He was thinking now he should have waited, given it more thought and picked another place. This seemed too close to Tel Aviv. They'd gotten here in twenty minutes. Maybe it should have been out somewhere in the desert, in the Negev. They drop the money and leave and he picked it up later. He should have taken more time. The guy, somebody, was knocking at the door. . . .

"It's open."

"MY NAME'S DAVIS. I've got something for Mr. Rosen."

"Show me your name's Davis," Rosen said. He closed the attaché case, bringing the top part down.

Davis saw the automatic pointing at him. Little 32-caliber Beretta, seven shots. Not a bad weapon if the man knew how to use it.

"Are you Mr. Rosen?"

"Let's see something with your name on it."

Davis dropped the canvas travel bag on the table. He dug his wallet out of his pocket, opened it, and held it out for Rosen to see his Marine Corps I.D. The man was too old for Tali. He couldn't see the two of them making it together. The man would be like her father. Davis wondered if he should take the Beretta away from him. No—leave him alone. The man was nervous and had a right to be.

"Who's the one in the car?"

Davis put his wallet back in his pocket. "Some guy thinks he's a friend of mine."

Rosen looked at him, stared for a moment. He didn't understand, but it wasn't something he was going to get into a discussion about. He said, "You know what it is you're bringing me?"

"Yes, sir. Money."

Davis got the alligator case out of the travel bag and reached over to lay it on top of Rosen's attaché case. He watched the man snap it open.

"You mind my asking, sir—your name's *Al* Rosen?"

"That's right."

"You weren't by any chance a third baseman?"

Rosen looked up at him, his hands on the case.

"You're about the right age," Davis said. "The one played for the Indians, made Most Valuable Player in, I think, '53. Hit forty-three home runs, led the league with a three thirty-six average."

"You want to know something? You're the first person over here's asked me that," Rosen said. "How old you think I was then?"

"I don't know. In your twenties?"

"He hit three thirty-six," Rosen said, "but Mickey Vernon led the league that year. Beat him out by oh-oh-one percentage point with a three thirty-seven."

"Yeah?" Davis was interested and more at ease. "I don't remember what happened to him after that. I was only about eleven."

"Rosen? He retired, thirty-one years of age. Greenberg, the sonofabitch, wouldn't give him any more than twenty-seven five to come back, and Rosen said fuck it. He was already in the brokerage business."

"Greenberg from the Tigers?"

"Yeah, he was general manager of the Indians then."

"I guess I don't recall that," Davis said.

"Yeah, well, I'm about ten years older than you are." Opening the alligator case, Rosen said, "So you remember Al Rosen, huh?"

He picked up a sheet of paper that was inside and his expression changed as he began reading it, squinting or frowning, Davis wasn't sure which. Something wasn't right. Davis stepped around to look in the case. There wasn't anywhere near two hundred thousand inside. Just a bunch of loose hundred-dollar bills.

"You know about this?" Rosen was staring at him again. "He sent five grand. That's all."

"You think I took it?"

"I'm asking if he said anything about it, if he told you what he was doing."

"No, sir. He put two hundred thousand in there yesterday. I watched him."

"You counted it?"

"He said how much it was. There were twenty packs of hundred-dollar bills."

"How long have you been working with Tali, getting the packages?"

"This was the third one," Davis said. "There were some letters other times."

Rosen held up the sheet of paper. "My lawyer says, 'I'm not sure we can trust the Marine.'"

Davis was used to standing on the front side of a desk, at ease or at attention. He made no comment. It was all right, because he felt much different with Mr. Rosen than he did with Mr. Bandy. He respected Mr. Rosen.

"My lawyer says we can't trust *anyone* under the circumstances. 'Anyone' underlined. He says, my lawyer who's been here two days, 'Let's consider this a test run. If you receive the five thousand intact we will know we have established a reliable liaison'—Jesus Christ—'and I will feel more confident in carrying out the responsibility of seeing that you receive the entire amount.'"

"He writes different than he talks," Davis said.

"Fucking lawyer," Rosen said. "His responsibility! It's not his responsibility, he's got nothing to do with the money!"

"Why don't you fire him?" Davis said.

"He says *if* I receive this and so on. He doesn't say anything about if I *don't* receive it. You notice that?" Rosen said. "All right, why wouldn't I receive it? One, you ran off with it. Two, I didn't show up here for some reason. But if I knew it was coming, what's the only reason I wouldn't be here?" Rosen waited.

Davis shook his head.

"Because I'd be fucking dead is what I'd be," Rosen said. "The sonofabitch, he's waiting to see if I stay alive before he delivers the two hundred. I've got to save my ass and he's concerned, he's worrying, he says he wants to feel confident about his responsibility!"

"Why don't I go back and get it?" Davis said.

Rosen looked at him and seemed surprised. "You mean right now? You'd do that for me?"

"He says he wants to establish a liaison. Well, let's show him it's established." He watched Rosen reach into the case and pick up some hundred-dollar bills. "No, I don't need any more. The thousand Mr. Bandy gave me'll cover it."

Rosen paused. "How long you think it'll take you?"

"Forty minutes. If Mr. Bandy's there and he's got it ready."

"He'll be ready," Rosen said. He went over to the phone that was on the counter separating the kitchen from the living-room area. He dialed a number and asked for the room.

Now the lawyer would get chewed out. Davis felt good about that and was anxious to hear it. He didn't want to appear to be listening, though. It wasn't any of

his business. Walking out on the balcony, he heard
Rosen say, "Tali, let me speak to Mel. . . . Yeah, he's
here. Everything's fine." His voice sounded calm; he
was in control, knew what he was going to say. The
man was all right. People trying to kill him, he still
seemed to have it pretty well together.

"Mel . . . I got your note. . . ." Rosen was listening;
then: "Mel . . ." not able to get a word in. Davis could
picture the lawyer with his hand in his light blue pants,
talking, looking up at the wall.

Davis was looking down five stories at the lime-
green Camaro, the racing stripe—he hadn't realized
the white stripe didn't extend over the roof of the car.
Just on the hood and the trunk. The car looked empty.
The black guy, his new buddy, wasn't inside.

"Mel, you're a wonderful person, I appreciate your
concern. . . . Of course not, I understand. . . ."

It surprised Davis, Mr. Rosen's tone, his patience.

There he was. The black guy was over toward the
far end of the parking lot standing by a car, leaning
against the side, bending down a little now, talking to
somebody in the car. One in front, behind the wheel,
one or two in the back seat.

". . . I understand, Mel, you don't want to delay
this any more than I do . . . Mel, would you just do
one thing for me? PUT THE FUCKING MONEY
IN A BOX AND HAVE IT READY . . . RIGHT
NOW!"

Davis heard the phone slammed down.

"There," Rosen said, quietly again.

"You better come out here," Davis said.

"What is it?"

"You know anybody owns a white BMW?"

TEDDY CASS was the driver. Valenzuela was in back with the worried- or sick-looking street kid, Mati Harari, who sat with his hands folded tight.

"He says he thinks it's the top floor," Valenzuela said. "Number 23?"

Mati nodded.

"No name of Rosen on the mailboxes," Rashad said. "Less it's in Jewish. There's a little elevator, one set of stairs, very dark. I think it looks good. You want to hand me something out of the trunk?"

"When the hot-rodder leaves," Valenzuela said.

"What do I do, he comes out?" Rashad said. "I'm standing there."

"No, you better get around the back of the building someplace, till he comes out," Valenzuela said. "He'll think you got tired and left."

"What about him?" Teddy Cass said, half turned on the seat, nodding at Mati.

"He's going with us," Valenzuela said. "He's gonna knock on the door for us."

"IT'S THE SAME CAR," Rosen said. "You can almost see the dents in the front end. Sonofabitch with an Arab thing over his head."

"He showed it to me," Davis said. "Jesus, I never had any idea. Guy trying to get you to like him."

"I'm not blaming you," Rosen said. He was standing away from the balcony railing so that he could just see the BMW past the flat cement surface. "You wouldn't have any way of knowing. Maybe—could they have seen you with Tali?"

"I guess that was it, in the lobby. We weren't together more than a minute."

"Then the colored guy sucks up, gets in your car," Rosen said. "The one in front, I think that's the young guy with the hair. I don't know his name. Val's probably in back. You see a guy looks like an off-duty cop, that's Val. Or a fucking linebacker, something like that."

"The colored guy said his name was Kamal Rashad."

"Yeah, they're getting these cute names now," Rosen said. "Alabama Arabians. Well, shit, I don't know—" He turned to go into the room and came around again and stood there.

Davis watched the black guy, Rashad, coming away from the BMW, past empty parking spaces, then go behind some other cars, walking toward the Camaro.

"Which one's your car?" Davis said.

"The black one, right near the walk." It was a Mercedes four-door sedan.

"They know it's yours?"

"I don't see how they could."

It was next to the Camaro. They could run, get to the cars—then what?

All the BMW had to do was back up and it would block the drive. There were shrubs along the street;

you couldn't run over the lawn to get out. Well, maybe, but you could get hung up on a bush.

If they sat here long enough the guys in the BMW would come up looking, assuming they wanted to kill Rosen and they knew he was upstairs.

Davis realized he was getting excited. It was a good feeling. Not being aware of it as a feeling, but thinking, figuring out a way to gain control and either neutralize the situation or kick ass.

One option—call the police.

There's a suspicious-looking white car down in the parking lot. Then what? An Israeli cop comes in his white car. But if they were serious and it was their business—the guys in the BMW—they were liable to shoot the cop. Davis tried to imagine calling the police and explaining it in English over the phone, telling a long story.

Or call the embassy. Get somebody there, after he explained it, to call the cops and explain it again, second-hand, in Hebrew. How long would it take? The black guy was opening the door of the Camaro now, getting his bag out, looking up at the building.

They'd be armed. They could be impatient—

"What'd he shoot at you with?" Davis said. "The colored guy."

"I don't know. Some kind of a pistol."

Davis went into the room and picked up the Beretta. "This fully loaded?"

"I checked it," Rosen said.

"You got more cartridges?"

"In the briefcase. With an extra clip."

The Beretta had a three-and-five-eighths-inch barrel that barely extended past Davis' knuckle when his finger was wrapped around the trigger guard. "Are you any good with it?"

"I've had it since I came here," Rosen said.

"Can you put the rounds where you want is what I'm asking," Davis said.

"I've fired it a few times, in the desert."

He probably couldn't hit the wall but would never admit it. "Makes a noise for a little thing, doesn't it? Well," Davis said, "I think, instead of us standing around scratching our asses, we might as well be doing something."

"Like what?" Rosen said.

He was nervous but controlling it. That was good. "You want to get out of here," Davis said. "How about if we get the police?"

"The pol*ice*? What do I say, these guys are annoying me? We're standing there looking at each other? Listen, these people, you put them in a position, they'd shoot the cops cold, no fucking around. I don't think you understand who these people are."

"I said *get* the cops. I didn't say call them and get into something we can't explain," Davis said. "No, we give your friends a little time to get out. Work it so you don't get mixed up in it and have to answer questions."

"How?"

"Take your money, whatever you're gonna take, go downstairs by the door, and wait. You see their car leave, watch which way it turns going out. You take off and head the other way."

"Where will you be?"

"Don't worry about it. Then, once you're clear, where do you think you'll go?"

"Jesus Christ, I'm standing here—I don't see how I'm going anywhere, for Christ's sake, three, four of them waiting down there—"

"Mr. Rosen, come on. You got it pretty much together," Davis said. "You don't want to lose it now. Tell me where you're likely to go."

"I guess Jerusalem"—calm again—"the King David."

"Okay, later on I'll give you a call, see how you made it."

Rosen was frowning at him again, trying to figure something out. "Whatever you're doing, this is still part of the grand Mel gave you?"

"You worry too much about money," Davis said.

HE WAITED on the balcony with the Beretta, the extra clip, and the box of cartridges, giving Rosen two minutes to get downstairs—seeing the black guy with his bag over by the BMW again; the driver with long hair out of the car on the other side; the black guy moving away then, starting across the lawn toward the side of the apartment building.

Davis planned his shots and when he began firing the Beretta—the sound coming suddenly, echoing in the afternoon, in the shadow of the building—he knew where he wanted to place the rounds and fired methodically, steadily, running the black guy back to the car

first, then creasing one off the roof of the car and seeing the guy with long hair duck out of sight. Four,
three, two, one more. He pulled out the clip and
pushed the spare one into the grip with the flat of his
hand and began firing at the open space of blacktop
close to the car—hoping someone was phoning the police by now—putting a couple of rounds into the
doors, but being careful to keep away from the engine
and windows. He didn't want to disable the car and he
didn't want to hit any of them on purpose. He had fired
on and killed people he didn't know before, but it
wasn't his purpose now to kill. He was throwing rocks
at crows in a planted field, getting them out of there; he
wasn't at Khe San or Da Nang or Hill 881. He reloaded
a clip and fired three rounds, then reloaded the second
clip before he emptied the first one and reloaded it
again. He heard the sirens, the irritating wail becoming
gradually louder. He waited, giving the guys in the car
time to hear it and think about it, then poured five
rounds hard into the flank of the white car. The car
was backing out. He was tempted to glance one off the
windshield, but it could fuck things up, delay them.
The siren wail was doing the job, the sounds coming
from different directions now. He fired two more shots,
changed clips, fired three times as the BMW backed up,
cutting hard, and emptied the clip at the taillight as the
car shot out the drive and turned right.

Rosen was outside . . . getting in his car.

Come on, get the fucker out of there! Quick!

Rosen made it. He was out the drive and on the
street, then taking his time—good—as three Israeli

police cars, sirens flashing, came screaming up Bilu toward the apartment building.

Davis used his shirt tail to wipe the grip of the Beretta. He dropped the gun and the extra clip and the box of cartridges over the side, down five floors into thick bushes.

A SQUAD CAR sealed him off before he got the door of the Camaro open. He asked them what the hell was going on, man. They patted him down and looked inside the Marine bag and asked to see his I.D. while squad cars came wailing in and police began swarming around the building. Davis gave them an anxious, bewildered look. They asked him if he lived here. He said no, he'd been visiting somebody. The shooting had started and he hadn't known if it was another war or her husband coming in the fucking door. Either way he was getting out of here.

He'd have told them more if they'd wanted to wait and listen.

11

THE MAN SEEMED to spend half his life in the bathroom. When Tali came back with his cigarettes—after looking around the lobby and then looking outside for Mati or the car, not knowing where he had parked it yesterday—Mr. Bandy was still in the bathroom, the one in 823. The only time he'd used the one in 824 was when he'd say to her, "Hold it, I got to piss," or, "I got to take a leak," telling her what he was going to do.

She thought about the Marine. Mr. Rosen had said yes, he was there, everything was fine. But she knew it wasn't fine, at least not everything, because Mati hadn't come back.

She thought of a friend of hers named Omri who worked for El Al as a flight security officer. He had shot a terrorist and arrested another during an attempted skyjack. It had been more than three years ago. She didn't know what Omri was doing now or why she thought of him. Maybe she wanted to see him again. Maybe the Marine reminded her of him, though they looked nothing alike.

Mr. Bandy confused her a little when he came into the room with the towel wrapped around his middle and carrying a magazine, which he threw on the couch. She could not understand why a man with his body would like to walk around half naked. Even people at the beach would look at him; he was so white. She had to pretend not to notice his nakedness.

"Your cigarettes are there on the table."

"I see them." He was making another drink, which he always did after bathing, before he got dressed.

"Those men weren't in the lobby," Tali said.

"They're probably still following what's-his-name." Now, as he always did, he sprawled on the couch and raised one of his legs to rest it on the cushion. She could see the fleshy insides of his thighs.

"It wouldn't take him that long to go to Jaffa and return," Tali said. "Even if he walk there." Mati was to go to the archeological excavation in the center of the tourist area and, when it appeared that no one was watching, drop the package into the dig.

"He's cruising Dizengoff in the Mercedes," Mel said. "Lining up some ass."

"He was suppose to come right back." Tali walked to the windows and watched the cars on Hayarkon. "Maybe they didn't follow him."

"Or maybe he took off," Mel said. "Rosie actually trusts him with a Mercedes?"

"Mr. Rosen bought a new one," Tali said. "He's going to sell the one we're using, when he tells me to advertise it in the *Post*." From the window, all the cars on the street looked the same. "Mati should be back," Tali said.

"You sleeping with Mati?"

"No, I don't sleep with him. He's a friend."

"Don't you sleep with friends?"

"I know Mati a long time, when I am teaching at the *ulpan* in Jerusalem, the language school for immigrants. Do you know the *ulpan*? Like an absorption center."

"I hope you weren't teaching him English."

"No, I taught Hebrew. Mati is Yemenite, but he was living with his family in Bayt Lahm—Bethlehem. Well, one day when Mati was much younger . . . the people there, this day they are Jordanian, the next day they are Israeli. In the '67 War." Tali gave her little shrug. "So we have a place, the *ulpan*, where we teach them Hebrew. Also people from Europe, from all over they come there. I did that when I moved from Beersheba and was going to the university."

"You teach Rosie Hebrew?"

"No"—she shook her head in a relaxed sweep, with an innocent expression, thinking of what she was going to say—"after my army service I went to work for El Al as an air hostess. That was where I met Mr. Rosen." She smiled. "He talk to me all the time from New York to Athens. Then I was with him again in a few days here at the Pal where he was staying. We talk some more." She was smiling again. "I laugh very much at the things he say. Then, no, it was weeks later I saw him at Mandy's Drugstore having dinner. He came over by us and asked me if I would work for him."

"To do what?"

"Be his secretary."

"You sleep with him?"

"No, I don't sleep with him." Irritated. "Why do you ask if I sleep with somebody? I sleep with who I want to."

"That's good," Mel said. "That's exactly the way it's supposed to be. You want to go to bed?"

"*No*, I don't want to go to bed."

"Don't you like to fuck?"

She said, "I enjoy to make love, but I do not like to simply, what you said, fuck. What is that? It should be a natural thing."

"What's the difference?" Mel said. "You're with somebody who doesn't turn you on all the way, close your eyes, pretend it's somebody else. You ever do that?" When she didn't answer he said, "Listen, I'm not talking about anything kinky. I don't mind it straight once in a while."

"I'm here to do work," Tali said. "Different things, if you want me to call on the telephone or write letters, or show you places in Tel Aviv. Mati or I would be very happy to drive you." She wanted to be honest without offending him. "But what is personal to me is not part of the work."

"Let's give it a little time," Mel said.

She didn't know what that meant. She wanted to tell him the man who came here yesterday was right. Mr. Bandy was like white dog shit. What did he say. A pile of it. If white dog shit could be selfish and never consider the feelings of others.

She wanted to be away from him and the sound of the air-conditioning and the room-service trays of dirty dishes sitting in the hall. She remained because of Mr. Rosen. In case he needed her. Or to learn something Mr. Rosen would want to know. She would do anything for Mr. Rosen.

"Well," Mel said. He got up and started across the room. "What's the Marine's name?"

"David."

"David. When David comes back tell him to wait."

"He's coming back here?"

"I may go downstairs for a while." He went into 823, unwrapping the towel.

THE BMW LOOKED like it had come over the border from Lebanon without stopping: bullet punctures all over the body, lights shot out front and rear. Only the glass had not been hit. In Valenzuela's mind, that made it the Marine who had been doing the shooting. Ross would have broken windows trying to hit somebody. But why the Marine?

They were somewhere in the Tel Aviv area—Ramat Gan, Rashad said—the BMW parked within the shell of a new building under construction, in semi-darkness, hidden from the street. Teddy Cass had gone to the railway station, about half a mile west—they had passed it—to see about renting a car. Rashad was in the back seat of the BMW with the Arab-looking kid, talking to him. Valenzuela was out of the car looking at the cement forms and footings, like a building codes inspector.

When Teddy came with the car, they'd switch the guns and explosives from the trunk of the BMW to the new one. It would be a temporary car, something to drive until they could pick up another car without numbers or a rental license plate. The man in the Hatikva Quarter who sold guns had said he could get them a good car. Maybe even an American model. He had looked at the BMW early this morning when they'd gone to pick up the Uzis and handguns and the C4. He had run his hand over the front-end dents and red paint on the grille—before the bullet holes were added—and said, "But it would cost you seven thousand lira a week." A grand. Deal, Rashad had said.

They'd leave the BMW here. Rashad might call the man he'd gotten it from and was paying five hundred a week to and tell him where to pick it up. Or he might not.

Rashad, talking to the Arab-looking kid now, said, "For true? They called the Black Panthers?"

Mati nodded solemnly. "They not the same thing as your Black Panthers are, but they called that name. There was a place, on King George Street in Jerusalem, we used to meet, go there and drink something and talk. Everyone knew it was the place of the Black Panthers."

"You ain't shitting me now, are you?" Rashad said.

"No, I'm not shitting you. We call ourselves that, the Sephardim, the dark-skin ones."

"Things the same all over," Rashad said.

"Giving you the shit," Mati said. "Throwing you in jail."

"Come on," Rashad said, "you done time?"

"Yes, in Jerusalem it was demonstrating. Last May."

"Just trying to make yourself heard, huh? Explain your beef?"

"We were in front of the Knesset to speak to Sapir, the minister of finance. The police come and beat us with clubs. In jail they treat us like animals, don't give us to eat any good food. Also Haifa, I went there before. They arrest me for robbing a rich tourist, stealing his camera and watch. Nine months, man, I was in Haifa."

Rashad said, "Hey, it's a kick, you know it? Meet somebody waaay over here deep in the same shit. Same everywhere you go, have to take the man's shit, huh? How about the man you work for? Keep pushing your head in it?"

"Mr. Rosen?" Mati shrugged. "He don't give me trouble."

"I was thinking of the one at the hotel," Rashad said. "Don't you work for him?"

"That one, he's a fat pig. He sits on your face."

"Yeah—I wonder why this Mr. Rosen would work for a man like that."

"No, the other way," Mati said. "The fat one work for Mr. Rosen."

"Unh-unh." Rashad shook his head. "The fat one was paying this Rosen some money, wasn't he?"

"Yes."

"So this Rosen works for the fat one. We can't understand it. See that gentleman out there? He was a friend of Mr. Rosen in the States, see. Hasn't seen him in a while. He wants to talk to Mr. Rosen, but the fat one don't want him to. You understand what I'm saying?"

"He wants to kill Mr. Rosen," Mati said.

"*No.* Who told you that? No, the fat one is controlling Mr. Rosen. Got him by the nuts, as we say. And that gentleman, he wants to talk to Mr. Rosen and tell him hey, nobody's mad at you, man. Come on home. See, the fat one's been giving Mr. Rosen some shit, messing up his head. This gentleman, Mr. Valenzuela, just wants to get it straightened out. But *shit*, now Mr. Rosen's got some crazy motherfucker wants to shoot and kill us."

"That Marine," Mati said.

"Yeah, you see any of us shoot back? No, we don't want to shoot Mr. Rosen. We want to talk to the man. But we don't know where he is."

He watched the Arab-looking kid chew on his lip, the kid sitting there covered with snow.

Valenzuela came over to the car, looking out toward the street.

"Here comes Teddy. Get Ali Baba out, we'll have a talk with him."

"We already talked," Rashad said. "Mati here's my buddy."

12

A CHIMNEY MADE of oil drums extended from the top floor of the Park Hotel to the ground: a chute for debris as they cleared out the gutted structure. Davis had read about the fire and forgotten it. He looked at the place now—it was strange—with a personal interest. He knew someone who had been in the hotel that night. A friend of his.

At six-fifteen Davis called the King David from a café on the square. They said they were sorry, there was no Mr. Rosen registered at the hotel. Davis said how about if he left his name and a phone number, in case Mr. Rosen checked in?

He sat at a sidewalk table with a Maccabee, watching the people who came out into the evening dusk, beginning to relax as he drank the beer, debriefing himself. The waiter came over and said there was a telephone call that must be for him.

"Hello."

"I couldn't believe it," Rosen said. "Jesus, how many shots did you fire?"

"Twenty-eight," Davis said. "Four clips. You made it all right, huh?"

"Looking back all the way," Rosen said. "Jesus, you don't fool around, do you? Where are you?"

"Netanya. I thought I'd stay here tonight and head north in the morning. What're you going to do now?"

"I just got here a few minutes ago. I'm gonna call Mel first and get a few things straightened out."

"I could go back to Tel Aviv, if you want," Davis said. "Pick up the money for you."

"No, I appreciate it, I really do—everything you've done," Rosen said. "But I'll work something out. It's my problem, something I've been living with. I appreciate it, though."

"I was wondering, driving here," Davis said. "You think your lawyer—you said he was waiting to see if you stay alive before he delivers the money. You think he could be helping them in any way? So he wouldn't have to pay you?"

"Well, it's not like he's paying," Rosen said. "It's my money, out of my company."

"Except it's cash, it doesn't have your name on it," Davis said. "I was wondering, what if he's trying to keep it for himself?"

"He's got to account to people in the company," Rosen said. "He can't just walk off with it. No, I don't think so."

"But what if it looks like he delivered it to you and you were killed after?" Davis said. "Nobody knows what happened to the money. Your lawyer says, 'I don't know, I paid him,' or, 'I sent it to him.' Only he still has it."

There was a silence.

"I can't see him sticking his neck out," Rosen said. "I don't think he's got the balls to pull something like that. What does he do with it? He'd have to get it out of the country. . . ."

"You've been getting it in," Davis said.

A silence again.

"No, I don't think so."

"Well, you know him better than I do," Davis said. "It was just something entered my mind." That was about all he had to say. He waited a moment. Rosen didn't say anything. "Well, let me wish you luck. I hope you make it okay." He listened to Rosen again telling him how much he sincerely appreciated everything, and that was it.

Davis got several copies of the *Courier-Journal* out of the car and brought them to the table. He'd have another beer, check the Kentucky high-school basketball tournament scores—"Tourney Trail"—look at the menu and decide if he wanted to eat here. Before too long he'd have to see about a hotel room.

Shelby County 74, Apollo 68
Paducah Tilghman 75, McCreary County 60
Edmonson County 77, Betsy Layne 72
Henry Clay 77, Ballard 74

Blue Devils over the Ballard Bruins, last year's state champions . . .

Harrison County 75, Green County 54

If they were on Rosen's ass and he was scared they
were going to take him out, why didn't he run?

Christian County 67, Ashland 63
Shawnee 85, Clay County 57

What would you do if you were Rosen?

He sat for several minutes staring at the cars moving past in the dusk, circling the parkway, before he got
up from the table, dug out a couple of ten-pound notes
for the waiter, and walked away. He'd get something to
eat in Jerusalem.

THE DESKMAN at the King David came back and said he
was sorry, but there was no Mr. Rosen registered.

Davis gave the deskman his name and said, "I'll be
right over there. See those chairs by the window?"

Fifteen minutes passed. Rosen walked up to him in
the dimly lighted corner of the lobby, Davis sitting low
in the easy chair, his legs stretched out, his white cap
low on his eyes. Rosen pulled a chair in closer and sat
down, looking out the window toward the illuminated
walls of Jerusalem's Old City.

"I thought I was just talking to you on the phone."

"The last time I was in this hotel," Davis said,
"Kissinger was here to visit Rabin. Some of us were
brought over to help with security."

"It was in August," Rosen said. "I remember, they

had this place, the whole block, roped off—you couldn't even use the pool in case his wife wanted to take a swim. They moved everybody out of the top two floors, I mean people with reservations—kicked them out. The manager says to me, 'I'm sorry for this inconvenience, Mr. Rosen. We've arranged for you to move to a room on the third floor.' I said, 'Mr. Fink, come on. Are you serious? I've been living here two and a half years, spending something like twenty thousand lira a month, this guy comes once or twice a year, you want to give my suite to some State Department flunkies? Fucking freeloaders?' I said, 'Mr. Fink, is this the world-renowned King David Hotel or a Howard Johnson's Motor Lodge?' I had a Secret Service man in the room all the time Kissinger was here, but I stayed."

"I was in the lobby, over there by the desk," Davis said. "Everybody's standing at attention, all the officials and dignitaries. Kissinger came in with Rabin's military adjutant and some of his aides. He stood there looking around. Just for a moment it was very quiet. And right then, in the silence, somebody let a fart."

"Come on—"

"That's my King David Hotel story."

"I bet I know who it was," Rosen said. "You come all the way to Jerusalem to tell me your King David Hotel story?"

"No, I wanted to ask you something," Davis said. "How come you haven't run? Left the country?"

"I would, but I don't have my passport," Rosen said.

"You lost it?"

"In a way. I know where it is, who's got it, but I'm having a little trouble locating the person."

"Go to the embassy, tell them you lost it."

"If I have to. I'll wait and see."

Davis was silent.

"You came all the way here to ask me that? You could've phoned."

"I came to make a suggestion," Davis said. "Something you might consider."

"Well, I'm certainly open to suggestions," Rosen said. "About all I can see to do right now is get in bed and pull the covers over my head."

"Did you call your lawyer?"

"We had a nice talk. I told him what happened and he said, 'See?' He said now they'd be coming back and hitting on him for not letting them know I called. I said, Mel, tell them who you work for, maybe they'll understand. Mel was very upset. I said shit, Mel, leave the money in the hotel safe and go home. Tell Shapira, the manager of the Pal, that I'll pick it up sometime. But he said no, he was gonna stick it out till I got the money. He said, but I wouldn't be able to come near the hotel without them seeing me." Rosen nodded, looking at Davis. "I know what you're gonna say and I couldn't help thinking the same thing. He doesn't want it out of his hands. He finds out I'm dead, the money's his. He goes home and tells them he paid me the day before I was shot. Christ. I don't know—you want a drink?"

"Not right now, unless you want one," Davis said.

"No, I don't care."

"You say your lawyer's nervous. What if they go see him again?" Davis said. "Rashad and . . . whoever they are."

"He's going to tell them what he comes all the way to Israel to tell me in person and ends up telling me over the phone," Rosen said. "I'm no longer president of my fucking company. That's what he tells me. They voted me out, these clucks on the board, guys I brought in. Let 'em buy a piece of the business. Mel says after three years of *carrying* me, they voted me a final payment, the two hundred grand and that's it, for my stock, everything. I can't bring suit because I'm not there. Two hundred grand, the fucking company's writing a hundred million dollars worth of home mortgages a year. . . ."

"That's what you're in, the mortgage business?"

"Mortgage broker," Rosen said. "We secure government-approved mortgages, usually on low-cost housing around Detroit, and sell them to out-of-state banks at one, one and a quarter percent."

"I don't understand anything about that," Davis said. "I never owned a home."

"It's paperwork. You hire bookkeepers and lawyers like Mel, the sonofabitch. He's gonna tell them—the guys you were shooting at—that he contacted me, yes, to tell me I'm out of the business, that's all. So he doesn't have anything more to do with me."

"He explained a little to me about you testifying against somebody in court," Davis said. "But I didn't understand much of that either."

"Well, I was doing some business with a guy named

Harry Manza. He was developing land, putting up these twenty-nine nine condominiums, you ever read American newspapers you've seen the ads, places with names like Apple Creek. There isn't a fucking apple tree in ten miles. Harry was also into a lot of other things, the federal government trying to nail him for a long time—years."

"This guy," Davis said, "he was in the Mafia?"

"I don't know, that's a word. You remember Al Rosen, you might've seen Harry Manza on TV about the same time, the Kefauver Committee, investigating organized crime."

"I think so, but I don't recall the name Harry Manza."

"Well, I knew something about Harry and about a guy that worked for him, Gene Valenzuela, who was one of the guys you were shooting at."

"You saw him in the car?"

"No, but Mel said it was Val came to see him. He's here to do the job on account of I did a job on him. At that time, it was three and a half years ago, the Justice Department wanted to get me on a very minor fraud technicality, but it was the kind of thing could ruin me, put me out of business. They'd drop the indictment, they said, if I'd let them wire me with a bug so they could listen to my luncheon conversations with Harry. You know what that's like, fucking wires taped on you, battery in your pocket? You're waiting for him to say, 'What's that sticking out of your shirt?' You say, 'Oh, it's my new hearing aid.' We'd have lunch, I couldn't even finish a plate of cottage cheese. Also, they wanted me to tell a grand jury what I knew about Harry and Val. They swore, the Justice Department, that the two guys would be put away practically forever." Rosen shrugged. "They never even came to trial."

"You were taking a chance," Davis said.

"Sure, I was taking a chance," Rosen said, "but I was highly motivated, I'll tell you. This guy, Harry Manza, had been wanting to buy a piece of my company. My associates said fine, because Harry scared the shit out of them. I said no fucking way I'm letting him in, I'll go out of business first. It was only a matter of time, I'm convinced, he would've had me killed."

"How do you know?"

"Because I saw it happen. There was a moving-and-storage company Harry wanted to buy into where the owner was killed in an explosion, in his warehouse. Harry played golf with the guy. He'd say to me, 'See, a man tried to do it all himself instead of cutting the pie. It can kill him.' Things like that. But never any reference to it when I was wearing the bug."

"That's what the police wanted him for?"

"The Justice Department, yes, first-degree murder, no fooling around, man, and I was gonna be their star witness. But as I said, after talking to the grand jury and all—Harry and Val *knowing* about it—they were never indicted. The only good thing that came out of it, Harry had a stroke and is practically bedridden. Val, a little later, served a few months for bribery, getting an FHA appraiser laid, some very minor rap, and now Val's in Israel for the shooting season."

"Gene Valenzuela, Kamal Rashad," Davis said. "How many others?"

"One I'm sure of," Rosen said. "Val had somebody with him when he saw Mel, but it wasn't the colored guy."

"Your lawyer said your car was blown up."

"That's right. Killed a guy from the gas station."

"And you say this other one, in the warehouse, was killed in an explosion."

"Yeah, it could be Val's got a dynamite man with him," Rosen said. "Mel said he was a young guy."

"They learn young in the war," Davis said.

"I keep forgetting to ask you," Rosen said, "if you hit anybody."

Davis shook his head. "It wasn't what I had in mind. One thing surprised me a little. Nobody returned fire."

"They wouldn't have come without guns," Rosen said, "if that's what you're thinking."

"No, I guess by the time they figured out where I was, they had to get out," Davis said. "Now they've got to start looking for you again. I imagine they'll go see your lawyer and ask him about it first. There's Tali—maybe Tali should stay out of sight for a while. What I'm saying is, they've got to talk to somebody to find out your habits, where you've been living. . . ."

"Go on," Rosen said.

". . . Where you're likely to be. Say they hire somebody to watch the airport. Or pay somebody at TWA and El Al to let them know if you're leaving. They don't know you lost your passport."

"No."

"They might know about the money, though. Your lawyer could tell them. So they could figure to use it as bait."

"Maybe. Shit, I don't know." Rosen paused. "You said you had a suggestion."

"How about if you called up this guy Val something and told him to get fucked?" Davis said.

"That's your suggestion?"

"Call him up, see if you can reason with him."

"Reason with him about what? Talk him out of it? This isn't an emotional thing with him, it's a score. And scores you settle."

"Well, this idea I've been thinking about," Davis said, "you may not feel comfortable with it, but I believe it could work."

Rosen hesitated, running a few options through his head, trying to anticipate the idea. "You're thinking, I can't reason with Val but maybe I could make a deal with him."

"Unh-unh."

"Pay him off."

"No, I was thinking you could kill him," Davis said. "Turn it around, hit him before he hits you."

13

THE WOMAN FROM Allentown, Pennsylvania, about sixty, said, "Christ, don't Jews drink? I walked all the way down Ben Yehuda to Frishman and back Dizengolf. If it was New York there'd have been two hundred bars."

She told Mel, sitting next to him in the Pal Hotel bar, that she was on the "We Are Here!" tour with a seventy-three-year-old woman named Dorothy who didn't drink or smoke and was always bitching and sniffing and fanning the air to rid it of cigarette fumes. The woman from Allentown told Mel she had eight grandchildren, that her husband was a steelworker at Bethlehem, and that she had found out recently her grandmother was illegitimate—honest to Christ—and her grandmother's father had been a Jew. It had shaken her up to find out she had Jewish blood, she said, and she was over here to learn something about the Jewish faith and see if she could buy any of it.

It was a change from sitting in the room. The

bartender, Itzak, would say, "Yes, please, Mr. Bondy," pouring Scotch, and serve up plates of olives, peanuts, and soft potato chips. The woman from Allentown, on her third VO and Coke, said if Dorothy didn't quit complaining about her smoking in the room, she was going to tell her to go fuck herself. Mel said to her, "You know who the piano player looks like? Sadat." He got a kick out of that, imagining Sadat moonlighting, flying over from Cairo each evening to play cocktail piano in Tel Aviv. The woman from Allentown said, "Who's Sadat?"

When he got upstairs, Mel let himself into 823. The adjoining room was dark, Tali asleep in the single bed next to the phone. She straightened as he reached the bed. He could see her face and a bare arm in the light from 823.

"I thought you were asleep."

"I was for a little while."

"You want me to get in with you?"

"No, I don't."

"I could've had a winner I was talking to at the bar, gorgeous broad. I came back to you." No response. "The Marine didn't come?" No. "Nobody called?" No one. "You want to just, uh, fool around a little? . . . Well, if you change your mind."

Mel went into 823, undressed, and got into bed. Maybe they had whores available. He should've checked at the bar. He was pretty sure Tali was sleeping naked; or maybe she had just her panties on, skimpy little briefs. He imagined the door creaking and seeing her naked body in the light from the window,

Tali saying softly, with her cute accent, "Can I come in with you, please, Mr. Bondy?"

The lamp was on when he opened his eyes. It wasn't Tali. It was the Marine, wearing a white cap, looking down at him.

"What the hell do you want?"

"Mr. Rosen's money. He sent me."

Mel squirmed up against the headboard, pulling the cover with him.

"You come in here, I'm sound asleep—where is he?"

"He said he'd just as soon I didn't tell anybody."

"Well listen, I told *him*, he wants the money he'd have to come get it," Mel said. "I'm not gonna get caught in the middle—those crazy nuts start shooting at each other. What is this, you work for him now? I thought you were on leave."

"I'm helping him out," Davis said.

"Yeah, well, have fun. You must be out of your mind."

"Instead of talking," Davis said, "why don't you give me the money and you can go back to sleep."

"I told him if he wants it, he can come get it. Until I hand it to him personally, it still belongs to the company. And if he doesn't pick it up, I take it back."

"When's that?"

"I haven't decided." Mel was settled again, in control. "Let me ask you something. You seem to be for hire. What if the guys who want Rosen paid you more?"

"More than what?"

"More than Rosen's paying you."

"Where are they? I'll talk to them."

Mel was studying him, realizing something for the first time. The Marine could put you on. He was low key and seemed to know what he was doing.

"Have they been back to see you?" Davis said.

Mel shook his head. "I don't have any idea where they are, but they're around. You realize," Mel said then, "you've got a very good chance of losing everything in this, and I mean your life. These guys don't fuck around, man. They don't go by any rules of war. They're close now, and they're going to stay on him, and I don't see how Rosie's got one fucking chance of making it." Mel paused. "Which leaves me with sort of a problem. A hundred and ninety-five thousand dollars. How do I get it home? I can find a way if I work on it, I'm sure. But you're leaving in a couple of weeks, I think you said. And you're allowed to ship all your personal gear?"

"Seventy-five hundred pounds," Davis said.

"Jesus Christ, what've you guys got?"

"In case you have a car, furniture, things like that," Davis said. "You're asking, if something happens to Mr. Rosen will I get the money home for you? Since I've been handling it, you might say?"

"It's an idea," Mel said.

"Deliver it in Detroit to Mr. Rosen's company?"

"Since he's not with the company anymore," Mel said, "you'd deliver it to my office."

"That's what I thought," Davis said.

"If there was about ten grand in it for you," Mel

said, "what difference would it make where you delivered it?"

"Why don't I take it now?"

"Why don't you think about it," Mel said, "and let me know. I'll be here. I'll be very interested to see how it works out."

As he spoke, Tali appeared in the connecting doorway sticking her shirttail in her jeans, zipping up. Davis glanced at her.

"Ready?"

She nodded and Mel said, "What is this? Where you going?"

"If you're only gonna sit around and wait to see who wins," Davis said, "you don't need Tali, do you?"

THEY CAME OUT of the hotel from the lighted entrance to early-morning darkness and walked along the aisles of parked cars looking for the gray Mercedes. She was worried about Mati again.

He had returned about eight o'clock and had acted strange, Tali said, keeping inside himself and saying very little about his trip to Jaffa with the package. Yes, they had followed him. Yes, it had gone all right. Well, where have you been? Oh, with friends. She couldn't stand that air of indifference.

Then she had forgotten about Mati because Mr. Rosen had called again, from Jerusalem, and spoken to Mr. Bandy for at least half an hour.

"He told you he was in Jerusalem?" Davis said.

"No, he didn't tell Mr. Bandy that," Tali said. "I

assume it. What he told Mr. Bandy was that he had lost his passport and that you were coming to pick up the money. Then Mr. Bandy spoke for a long time."

"Why did he tell him about his passport?"

"I don't know," Tali said. "It was only one of the things. I could hear Mr. Rosen's voice speaking loud at Mr. Bandy and Mr. Bandy would speak loud back at him. Then, after that, Mr. Bandy asked me questions about Mr. Rosen, about where he lived and spent his time. Then I look for Mati and he was gone."

Mati was gone and so was the gray Mercedes.

She was tense, asking him about Mr. Rosen as they drove in Raymond Garcia's Camaro to her apartment on Hamedina Square—to pack a few clothes—and didn't begin to relax until they had fixed coffee and were talking quietly on the terrace, Davis telling her Mr. Rosen was fine, giving her details about his meeting with Rosen and what had happened, where he was now, but not telling her what they planned to do. Davis wasn't sure himself about that part. He had the beginning of an idea. He could picture a controlled situation, a showdown, and could hope to steer them toward it. But he wasn't sure yet of Rosen, to what extent he could count on him. It was strange, getting excited about another man's problem as if it were his own.

He was aware of the darkness beyond the fifth-floor terrace, the dark sky and the dark shapes of buildings. The only lights were the streetlights, below, outlining Hamedina Square. He was aware of the girl also, and of another strange feeling—wanting to hold her and touch her face. He wasn't sure the feeling was sympathy.

"You and Mr. Rosen seem to get along pretty well."

"Yes, I like very much working for him," Tali said. "He's not here, I feel short. Is that what you say? I miss him. He's a very nice person."

"Like a father?"

"Yes, in a way. But the relation is different. He's more fun than a father is."

"Fun in what way?" He felt as if he were prying now.

"Fun because he says funny things. He doesn't laugh, but you know he's being funny. Do you understand?"

He understood. He had caught glimpses of it, but hadn't met the all-out funny Rosen yet. Maybe he never would.

DAVIS MADE a swing north out of Tel Aviv, through the empty, early-morning streets, to the Marine House. Tali waited in the Camaro, engine rumbling, while he ran inside and up to his room. Davis didn't bother with lights. He reached into a drawer and dug out the shoulder holster with the straps wrapped around it and the Colt .38 automatic wedged snugly inside. Also a box of ammo. He then crept across the hall to the room of Willard Mims, the 1st Force Recon Marine—over to the footlocker in the walk-in closet—and was almost out again when Willard opened his eyes and caught him at the door.

"Who's that?"

"It's just me, Willard. I didn't want to wake you up."

"What've you got there?"

"I just want to borrow a couple of your claymores. I'll pay you back."

"You'll pay me *back*—how? I brought them all the way from Da Nang."

"Willard, you don't happen to have any grenades, do you?"

"Jesus Christ—" Willard yanked at the sheet to throw it aside.

"Hey, never mind. Trust me, buddy. Okay?"

He was down the stairs, out of there, taking off in the Camaro before Willard got his feet on the floor.

Tali looked to see what he had thrown on the back seat: the holstered gun and the dull, heavy-looking metal objects that were about an inch thick and the size and shape of curved license plates. She thought she recognized them, but wasn't sure.

"Are those explosives?" Surprised.

"Claymore mines. All wired and ready to go."

"You have them at your house?"

"Not officially," Davis said. "This one boy, Willard, keeps some in his closet. I think he's a little crazy." They were silent and he didn't add until some moments later, "But I'm glad he's on our side."

14

THEY CAME to Jerusalem in Rosen's gray Mercedes: Rashad in front with his buddy Mati, who was driving; Valenzuela and Teddy Cass in the back seat; Valenzuela with his map open; the Uzis, Berettas, and plastic C4 explosives in the trunk. Rashad's idea: what'd they need to spend a grand a week on a car for when Mati had the man's? Bring Mati into the club along with the Mercedes. They all had to smile at the idea of using Rosen's own car. They hoped Rosen would have time to realize it.

At seven A.M. they topped the rise, coming up out of the switchbacks of the mountain road, and coasted down into the city, the street narrowing and curving, buildings of tan-rose Jerusalem stone rising on both sides, through an old section of the city, catching glimpses of modern high-rises in the distance—clean in morning sunlight—Valenzuela looking from the blue street signs on buildings to his map; then taking a curve off Yafo, the Jaffa Road, past the Hebrew Union College to the King David.

"There," Mati said, slowing down, creeping past the plain, stone, squared-off structure that rose six stories and was topped off by two additional, newer floors.

"That's it, huh?" Valenzuela said. "It looks like a YMCA."

"The YMCA is across the street," Mati said, a little surprised.

"The YMCA looks like what the King David should look like," Rashad said. "Where they keep the cars?"

Mati pointed. "There."

"Turn in."

The Mercedes turned left into a side street and left again through the open gate of a chain-link fence, past a booth where the parking attendant sat. There were no more than a dozen cars in the lot, in two irregular rows, most of them at the fence toward the front, facing the street.

"You see his car?" Rashad said.

"That one," Mati said.

"Yeah, I remember it now," Rashad said. "It was out in front of the apartment. Pull in next to it." When they came to a stop parallel with the black Mercedes, he said, "Who's going in?"

"I am," Valenzuela said. "And you and your friend. Teddy'll wait here."

Mati said, "It would be good, I go talk to him first."

"It would be bad," Valenzuela said. "Teddy, open the trunk."

FROM THE PORTE COCHERE of the main entrance they passed single file through the revolving door and went past rows of tour-group luggage being assembled opposite the registration desk, Valenzuela carrying a black vinyl briefcase, followed by Mati and Rashad.

"What way?"

"To, that way," Mati pointed.

They turned right, went past the desk to the elevator.

On the seventh floor they turned right again and walked down the hall to 732. Next to it, on the floor, was a tray on which sat two glasses, an empty champagne bottle, and an ashtray heaped with cigarette butts. Valenzuela nodded. Mati approached the door, cleared his throat, and knocked lightly, twice.

"Hit it harder," Valenzuela said.

Mati knocked again, rapping quickly with his knuckles. They waited.

"Once more," Valenzuela said.

Mati knocked several more times. Cautiously, Rashad leaned in, pressing his head against the door. He came away, looked at Valenzuela, and shrugged.

"Okay," Valenzuela said. Moving away, he looked down at the tray. "He was always neat, I remember that. Couple of times we visited him at his office, he was always getting up and emptying the ashtrays."

In the elevator, Rashad said, "What do you think?"

"I think somebody's in there with him," Valenzuela said. "I don't want to do it that way if I can avoid it. If I can't, if it's a broad, somebody like that who's gonna be with him, then it's too bad, there isn't anything I can do about it."

"Maybe it's the Marine," Rashad said.

"I hope so," Valenzuela said.

"DIDN'T YOU HEAR IT?" Edie said.

"It's the maid," Rosen said. He opened the door to the sitting room and listened a moment. "They like to come in and make the bed while you're still in it."

"You're sure it's the maid?"

"Well, it isn't the guy I'm meeting, the one I mentioned to you. We've got a signal."

"Something's going on," Edie said. "I don't understand at all. Who are you trying to avoid?"

She looked cute frowning, pouting a little. Forty-something years old, but she could put on a cute pose and get away with it. She was tanner than before, very tan with the white sheet pulled up around her.

"I told you," Rosen said, "somebody I don't want to do business with's been pestering me . . . an insurance salesman." That was it. "You know the type I mean? Won't take no?"

Rosen was in his light blue nylon Jockeys this morning. He hadn't eaten lunch or dinner yesterday and he felt very thin, with no need to hold himself in. He had jumped up at the sound of the first knock on the door, calmed himself, gone into the bathroom, and brushed his teeth. Now he got back in bed, and, very gently, pushed Edie down next to him. She looked good first thing in the morning.

"You ever wear curlers in your hair?"

"Not when it's short like this. When it's longer I have it done."

"I like it. My wife used to wear pink curlers and a hairnet."

"You're *mar*ried?" She started to sit up and he had to hold her down.

"No, *when* we were married she wore the curlers. She got a divorce right after I came here. No-fault, no argument, cash settlement. She wouldn't have lasted here a week."

"I love it here," Edie said. "I feel so . . . different. I'm in your bed and I didn't even know if you were married or single."

"Swinging singles, that's us. So . . . we'll get to know each other. Let it all hang out."

"After you finish your business." With just a slight edge to her tone.

"I'm sincerely, really sorry," Rosen said. "If I could put it off, I would. But I've *got* to spend some time with this guy. He's gone out of his way, doing me a considerable favor. I can't very well tell him hey, wait till I get back from a trip I want to take. You understand?"

"No, I don't understand. You haven't told me anything," Edie said, with the little-girl pout again. It was cute now and he wondered if it would always be cute. Like things his wife had used to do. Dumb little things that finally began to irritate him. The way she used to sit perched on a chair with her back arched and her legs tucked under her, trying to look cute. Or the way she used to put on a little scatterbrained act being cute and saying oh well, she guessed she was just a little kooky. She wasn't kooky. She was purebred suburban Detroit and didn't know what kooky was. After a while he couldn't stand any overweight woman who tried to act like a little girl. Edie was thin and firm. There was no reason now, at her age, she would ever put on weight. She was nice; she was just trying a few things on him, a few leftover poses. Maybe they were all still little girls in there. How old was *he?* Shit, about nineteen.

"If I'd wanted to avoid you," Rosen said, "would I have called the hotels, the embassy, your home . . . talked to your daughter?"

"You just wanted your passport."

"That reminds me. . . ."

"It's at the hotel. God, what time is it?"

"A little after seven. You've got plenty of time."

"They said to be ready by nine. The bus leaves promptly at nine-fifteen for the airport."

"Don't worry, I'll get you to the hotel," Rosen said. "I promise." Softly then, "Edie? Let's not talk for a while." He began to nibble at her shoulder.

She turned, moving her body against his. She said, "You only wanted your passport," but it was a nice tone now, subdued.

"If that was all I wanted," Rosen said, "when I called the Dan I would've left a message, leave it at the desk, I'll pick it up. No, I asked that you call me, didn't I?"

"I never wanted to see you again," Edie said. "I rushed back to Netanya, took a cab. . . ."

"I know, I should've left word," soothing her. "I thought I'd be right back, but . . . things developed." They had been all through this. Rosen was patient, though; he wasn't going anywhere in the next hour and a half.

"You don't know how I looked forward to it," Edie said, "traveling together, seeing Israel with you."

"I know," Rosen said. "So did I. And we will, I promise."

Last night, after the Marine had left, Rosen had gone into the bar for a nightcap with Silva, turned on the stool to leave, and there she was—sitting right beyond the electric keyboard with three women—staring at him.

The first part wasn't easy, even with his enthusiasm, being glad to see her, rushing over and kissing her, smiling as he was introduced to the "Hadassah Holiday" ladies, then practically forcing her, with her clenched expression, to go with him to the garden . . . to talk, to get a few things straightened out. It was hard work. Women could be stubborn and have to be persuaded nicely to do things they wanted to do. Usually it was a pain in the ass, but last night it had been worth the effort. His passport was in her room at the Hilton. He had her with him and knew he'd get his passport. Then showing her his suite, his home away from home, and ordering the champagne and two packs of Winstons. He liked very much making love to her. He was himself and it was a lot of fun. He told her that and she said she felt the same thing; she felt free and, for some reason, not at all self-conscious or inhibited. See? Rosen said. They were meant for each other and nothing was going to keep them apart. Except for the few days he'd have to spend on business. Her tour was flying south to Eilat, to visit Solomon's Pillars and the Red Sea. Okay, he'd meet her there at the Laromme. If for any reason he couldn't make it, he'd call. But they would definitely meet somewhere before the end of her tour and make plans from there.

"The ladies in the group," Edie said, "they're going to give me funny looks when I show up."

"Tell them you're in love," Rosen said.

"I'll tell them I spent the night with you because it was God's will," Edie said. "How have you and God been getting along?"

"My God," Rosen said. "Tell you the truth, I haven't been thinking about it lately."

As a matter of fact, he hadn't thought about his Will of God theory since the night of the hotel fire. It went through his mind: What would God think of him shooting Gene Valenzuela if he got the chance?

The answer was there immediately: He'd probably love it.

MATI CAME away from the hotel parking attendant to the spot where they were standing behind the gray Mercedes.

"He said Mr. Rosen always come and get his car himself."

Valenzuela said, "Did he ask you anything? Why you wanted to know?"

"No, I told him, as you said, you hire me to drive you, to see Mr. Rosen. You want to know is his car here or did he call to have it brought."

Valenzuela looked at Teddy Cass. "How long will it take you?"

"Few minutes, that's all. But it should look like we're doing something."

"We'll jack this one up." Valenzuela put his hand on the trunk lid of the gray Mercedes. "Look like we're changing the right rear. Mati can do that for us."

Mati didn't understand. "You want the tire change?"

"Jack it up, we'll do the rest," Valenzuela said. He turned to Rashad. "Then you and Mati go get a cup of coffee, have a talk. Right?" He pulled the map out of his coat pocket, unfolded it, looked at arrows and circles drawn in ink, and said, "We'll meet you around on Agron Street. Corner of Agron and . . . Ben Shimon."

Mati didn't say anything until they came out of the parking lot and started up the street past the hotel.

"They going to blow him up."

Rashad said, "They do that in Jerusalem, man, not in the civilized world of business."

"Yes, they do it in Jerusalem," Mati said. "So another bomb, they think, oh, the terrorists again, trying to kill Jews. They look for Arabs, they don't look for Americans."

"We're gonna have another talk over a cup of sweet

Turkish," Rashad said. "Man, I think I get through to you, explain how the situation is, you still worrying."

"Mr. Rosen never done nothing to me," Mati said.

"He never done nothing to me either," Rashad said, "but he done things to other people—with his money, sending people to jail. With his money, frightening an old man till he had a heart attack and almost died. Man, come on, you see a pile of shit, you don't have to be sitting in it to know it's shit, do you?"

Mati was shaking his head. "I don't know. . . ."

"I know you don't," Rashad said, "that's why I'm explaining it to you. You want to change things, clean up the shit put there by people who like to stick you in it. It's the same thing, man, what we're doing. You got to scare them a little, don't you? Get their attention? Sure, he sees his fine automobile blow up, he says, 'Hey, maybe I better have a talk with them. They serious.' "

"You not going to kill him?"

"Noooo, man, I been telling you, we gonna talk to him, get his reactions. What we want you to do is go back to Tel Aviv and keep an eye on the fatty. You think you can get a bus or something?"

"I have Mr. Rosen's car."

"No, we're gonna use it, buddy. Case we have to be some place in a hurry. What you do, tell Mr. Bandy you gave Mr. Rosen back his car, he wanted it for something. Then you try and stay close to Mr. Bandy if you can. See, Mr. Rosen may not be here. We don't know for sure. And he may call Mr. Bandy and let him know where he is. You understand?"

"Yes." Mati nodded.

"Mr. Rosen wants his money, don't he?"

Mati nodded again. "And his passport."

"Say what?" Rashad said.

"I hear Tali talk to Mr. Bandy about the money and about he lost his passport. When I went back last night."

"You don't mean to tell me," Rashad said. "You keeping that a secret?"

"I didn't think of it before."

"Okay. So you stay with Mr. Bandy," Rashad said. "Tell him you'll rent a car for him if he wants to go some place. See, then if we want to get in touch with you, find out anything, we call the hotel. So you got to stay close, like in the lobby."

"What if he don't need me? The fat one," Mati said.

"No, my man, *we* the ones need you," Rashad said, putting an arm around Mati's thin shoulders as they walked along David Ha-Melekh Street past the hotel. "You on the team now."

15

IN THE CAMARO, in the hills west of Jerusalem, Tali said, "Do you miss war? Is that it? You miss the screechy, the excitement?"

Davis kept his eyes on the road. "No, I don't miss war."

"Then what are you doing this for? You don't want to protect him. You want to have war with *them*."

"I don't think he has a choice," Davis said. "If you look at it."

"He can wait for them to go. Hide some place they never find him."

"He's tired of hiding," Davis said. "He's been hiding for three years. He thinks he wants to go home, but he's afraid to stick his head out. He's tired of looking over his shoulder and now he sees a chance to end it."

"Why are you helping him?"

"Because he doesn't know how to do it himself."

"That's the only reason? Not for yourself?"

"What do you mean, for money?"

"No, it's why I ask you," Tali said, "do you miss war? Why else do you want to kill someone?"

"Why do you fight wars? Your country," Davis said.

"Because they attack us."

"It's the same thing."

"No, it isn't," Tali said.

Following the switchbacks, in morning shade, he tried to think of things to say and told her about an Israeli friend of his named Zohar who lived near the Marine House and would see them "making gymnastics in the morning"—jogging. Zohar had lived in Eilat for six years, and when he'd moved north with his family, coming from the Sinai desert, he'd said, "We had starvation in our eyes for the green." So they'd bought a house in the trees near Herzliya Pituah.

He told her about visiting Jerusalem the first time, with Zohar, and Zohar showing him where his tank—and the tank of his good friend who was now the Hertz manager in Jerusalem—had been surrounded by Jordanians during the Six Days' War . . . showing him an archway that was like a stone tunnel in a gate and asking Davis if he thought a tank would fit through it—with the Jordanians firing rockets at them—because if the tank became stuck in there . . . but they had to try it and they did get through, barely, scraping the walls. Zohar showed him, in the side of a stucco house, an S-curve of bullet marks he had put there with his Uzi, firing out of the turret of his tank. He had brought his wife and three children here several times on outings. Davis said if he were married and had a family it would be like taking them to Da Nang and Lon Thien. He couldn't imagine it.

Tali said, "You're not married?"

"I almost was a couple of times," Davis said. "I was sort of engaged. But I'd get sent somewhere and by the time I'd get back I wouldn't be engaged anymore."

"When I was eighteen I was in love with an American who was going to dentist school," Tali said. "Do you know Atlanta? That's where he live. I visit him there, but"—she shrugged—"we write to each other for a while, but then we don't write anymore."

"I don't think you have to worry," Davis said.

"About what?"

"About meeting somebody and getting married."

"I don't know—I think I like to be an air hostess again and travel places."

"Maybe, while I'm still here," Davis said, "you could show me Israel. I haven't seen too much."

"Maybe. I don't know."

He wondered if she understood what he meant: traveling with him, staying at hotels with him.

They were on Yafo, in the middle of the morning traffic, when Tali saw Mati and told Davis to stop quick. He couldn't, though, for another half block. When he was able to pull to the curb, Tali jumped out, ran across the street through the traffic, and was gone. Davis waited, looking around. About ten minutes passed before he saw her again, recrossing the street with Mati now, scowling, yelling at him—that thin, nice-looking little girl—giving him hell in Hebrew as they approached the car and Davis leaned over to open the door.

"Mati and I have to have a talk," Tali said.

"Well, get in."

She pushed Mati into the back seat, got in front, and sat half turned, staring at him. "He says he drove them to the King David," Tali said, "but Mr. Rosen wasn't in his room. He says he was with them yesterday, they took him, when you were shooting at them."

"How many, three? Three men?"

Mati nodded.

"Where are they?"

"He says he doesn't know. They told him to go back to Tel Aviv. They kept Mr. Rosen's car." She began railing at Mati again in Hebrew, Mati sitting quietly with the holstered automatic and the claymore mines on the seat next to him, not aware of them, staring back at Tali. He ducked aside then as she tried to hit him with her fist. Davis caught her arm.

"Take it easy. Let's find out what happened."

"He's an idiot!" Tali said. "He thinks they only want to talk to Mr. Rosen." She lashed out at him again in Hebrew and this time Mati yelled back at her.

"Where did they go when they left him?" Davis said. "Where were they?"

They spoke again in Hebrew before Tali said, "At the hotel. He went with the black one to a café, then the black one left."

"The other two," Davis said, "they waited at the hotel?"

"They were in the parking lot by the car," Tali said.

She spoke to Mati again in Hebrew. Mati said something to her. "He says they wanted to change a tire. He raised the car for them. . . ."

"Which car?"

"The one he drove," Tali said. "But he says there was nothing wrong with the tire."

Davis had the Camaro in gear, cranking the wheel away from the curb.

"Parked next to Mr. Rosen's new car, the black one," Tali said.

Davis knew that before she told him.

"THE LAROMME'S the best hotel in Eilat," Rosen said. "It's big and flashy and you can get lost looking for the discotheque, but it's a lot of fun—if you don't get taken. A lot of good-looking young Israeli guys prey on tourist ladies, you know. It's like Rome."

"It's like anywhere," Edie said. "There was one at the Dan, I told him I was old enough to be his mother. Do you know what he said?"

"Just a second." Rosen stepped over to the desk, handed the clerk his key, and spoke to him for a moment. The clerk laughed. Rosen came back smiling at Edie and put his hand out to let her go first through the revolving door.

"What'd he say? The Israeli kid."

"He said . . ."

By now Rosen was talking to the doorman, handing him a lira, and the doorman was laughing.

"I'm sorry, go on."

Walking from the porte cochere down the circular drive to the street, Edie said the young Israeli's reply wasn't that much really. He'd only said he was in love with her and it didn't matter how old she was. Rosen said he didn't care how old she was either. What was age? What did it have to do with how you felt? Edie said, "Careful. I have your passport, you know. With your date of birth on it." Rosen said, "Oh . . . that's right."

Eight thirty-five. They'd get to the Hilton and have time for a cup of coffee.

"I have to change," Edie said.

"Then we'll have it while you change. I'll help you dress," Rosen said. "I'll help you undress first."

"You know, you're very sexy for a man your age," Edie said.

"Tourist ladies who stay at the Hilton like that kind of talk," Rosen said. "It excites them and their thing gets moist and tingles. You're not really a Hilton lady, though. Did I explain that to you? The difference between the Hilton ladies and the King David ladies?"

"No, but I can imagine what you're going to say."

She waited again as he stopped to talk to the parking lot attendant and press something into his hand. When he joined her again, taking her arm and squeezing it, she said, "I'll bet you over-tip."

"Of course," Rosen said.

THEY COULD HEAR boys playing basketball in the yard of the YMCA—voices in Hebrew, the sound of the ball hitting the backboard—beyond a wall of bushes and a high chain-link fence. The gray Mercedes was parked next to the fence, on Lincoln Street.

They'd hear it all right, Teddy Cass said. Shit, it would break windows in the Y.

But they wouldn't hear it if it didn't go off, Valenzuela said.

They had picked up Rashad on Agron Street and crept through the area in the Mercedes, studying side streets and through routes that Valenzuela had marked on his map. They had been here now a little more than forty minutes . . . almost forty-five minutes when they saw Rashad coming toward them from the front of the YMCA.

"Just leaving the hotel," Rashad said. "Going to the parking lot."

"Alone?" Valenzuela said.

"Has a woman with him."

"Well, there's nothing I can do about that," Valenzuela said.

THE KING DAVID parking lot attendant was always glad to see Mr. Rosen. Especially with a woman. When Mr. Rosen was alone, he gave him five lira. But when he was with a woman, he gave him ten lira. It couldn't be to impress the woman; she couldn't see the notes. So it must be because Mr. Rosen felt good and was happy. Why shouldn't he be happy? With money and two cars. One of the cars was gone now, taken by the Americans; but the new black one should be enough for him. He watched Mr. Rosen open the door for the woman and come around to this side to get in.

The sound the parking lot attendant heard at that moment was like a racing car streaking down David Ha-Melekh past the hotel, a roar of power, a screeching sound that made him grit his teeth waiting for the crash. But the sound that came was the engine roar again, higher, much louder, *here*, a green car power-sliding through the gate into the yard, raising a wave of dust and throwing gravel at him as the car swerved and came to a stop broadside. A man wearing a cap was out of the car almost as it stopped sliding.

"Rosen!"

Rosen took his hand from the ignition, looking out the side window at the Marine coming toward him and now Tali, behind him, getting out of the Camaro, and someone else. He didn't recognize Mati right away.

"That's the guy I was telling you about," Rosen said.

"My God," Edie said, "he makes an entrance."

Rosen grinned at the Marine. "What're you, out hot-rodding?"

Davis said, "Don't touch the ignition. You better get out of the car. Both of you."

"Jesus Christ," Rosen said. Rosen knew. He didn't have to ask questions. "Edie, come on."

"What is it?"

"We have to get out of here."

"Take the parking guy with you," Davis said. He waved to Tali and Mati to move back.

"You know what to do?" Rosen asked him. He was out of the car now.

"If I recognize it," Davis said. "Go all the way out to the street."

He didn't wait for them to leave. Getting down on his back, inching under the car, he heard the lady with Rosen asking him what was going on. The lady would have found out if Rosen had turned the key and the car had exploded beneath them. There were two fist-sized packs of C4 plastic wedged between the undercarriage and one of the frame cross members—one pack would have done the job—like hunks of white modeling clay, with wires and blasting caps attached. Davis pulled the caps out of the plastic material and put them in his pocket before he cut the wires with his clasp knife and pulled the hunks of plastic free.

They were outside the gate on the side street, watching him as he came out from under the car.

He tossed the hunks of plastic in the back seat of the Camaro, got behind the wheel, and drove toward them, seeing them walking into the lot again, stepping out of the way. Rosen hurried toward him.

"Get in," Davis said. "We've got to move."

"Wait a minute—what was it?" Rosen was frowning. It was happening too fast for him. He wasn't used to reacting, not asking questions.

"We don't have time to talk. Get in," Davis said.

"I don't have anything with me. . . ."

The good-looking lady with Rosen was saying,

"Will somebody tell me what's going on? What was under the car?"

"Wait a minute," Rosen said, his hands hitting the pockets of the light jacket he was wearing. "I don't have any money with me . . . my sunglasses . . ." With his beard and hair and blue choker beads, his indecision seemed out of character, weakness showing through.

Tali knew what was going on, her eyes on Davis, staring at him. Mati was a little behind her, alert or asleep, it was hard to tell.

"—Or my clothes. I've got to pack something."

"Mr. Rosen," Davis said, "forget about your clothes. Just get in the car."

Tali said, "What way are you going?"

"South. Stay here till we call you."

"To Beersheba?"

"At least. If we ever get out of here."

Rosen was in the car now, slamming the door. The lady, through the window, looked bewildered. Tali was calm.

"Or Eilat," Davis said. "Maybe you can drive down tomorrow, bring him some clothes."

"Where?"

"I don't know. The Laromme, I guess. We gotta go."

Rosen was leaning close to Davis to look out his side window. "Edie—talk to the girl, Tali. Listen, I'm gonna meet you, so be there. Okay?" And his parting words: "Edie—don't forget my passport!"

Tali watched the Camaro turn out of the lot, the lime-green screamer revving with a howl, and turn again, with a sound of squealing rubber, south onto David Ha-Melekh. She could still hear the car going through its gears, winding up, when it was out of sight ... and then the gray Mercedes shot past the lot, streaking in the same direction.

16

THREE HOURS SOUTH of Jerusalem, somewhere in the Negev, they were keeping the green Camaro in sight: four hundred yards, whatever it was, ahead of them, a speck, a dot on the road. Sooner or later the Camaro would falter or run out of gas or try to hide and they would have them. Rosen and the Marine. It had to be the Marine driving.

Valenzuela would stare at the road—past Rashad and Teddy Cass in the front seat—at the two-lane highway that could have been drawn with a ruler and seemed to extend into infinity, through flat desert landscape, colorless or dry brown and tinted in washed-out, dusty green. Dead land, with the Dead Sea somewhere to the east, left behind. Valenzuela would look from the road to the map that lay open on his legs.

They'd have them pretty soon.

There were only two roads south. One that followed the Jordanian border, and this one that linked the cities of the Negev. Eighty-five kilometers lined with young eucalyptus trees to Beersheba, where they had twice almost overtaken the Camaro scrambling through traffic, running red lights on the boulevard and out past the Arab market. Another twenty-seven miles to Dimona, the gray Mercedes continuing east past the mills and potassium works to follow the highway; then not seeing the Camaro and turning abruptly, realizing the Camaro had taken a secondary road due south out of Dimona, and finally seeing its dust hanging in the air on the way to Mizpeh Ramon.

They were now two hundred thirty-seven kilometers south of Jerusalem, about one hundred forty-five miles. According to Valenzuela's map, there were no through roads, nothing, no destination south of Mizpeh Ramon except Eilat, the Israeli port on the Gulf of Aqaba. Valenzuela liked the way it was working out, but he was getting anxious.

He said, "This would be a good place, along here."

Rashad raised his face to the side. "On the pavement this thing don't have it. Now it's hard to steer around the holes."

"Needs a tune," Valenzuela said. "The cheap fuck, all the money he's got."

"NO, THE WAY it was with medals," Davis said, "it was something you thought about *after*. You didn't go out to earn one, get decorated, unless you were pretty gungy, or crazy. In Vietnam, for instance, some guys were grabbing all the medals they could get. But, see, there was an inflation of medals there. NCOs and field-grade officers were writing them up for each other and you couldn't really tell the value, you know, unless a guy dove on a grenade, something like that. You see a lance corporal with a Silver Star, a major might've done the same thing and gotten the Congressional Medal of Honor. It's the way it was."

Rosen was half turned, looking back over the seat rest to the rear window. He was nervous and excited and had been talkative.

"I think they're gaining a little."

"I see them," Davis said. "We're all right." He was staying approximately five hundred meters ahead of the Mercedes, bringing them along, making sure they didn't get lost.

The road was no more than four meters wide, narrow strips of patched and broken pavement that would end abruptly and continue as rutted tracks of gravel for miles before the pavement would suddenly reappear, a roadway, some poured concrete and telephone lines, the only sign anyone had ever been here. The rest was desert scrub and bleached rock.

Davis held the Camaro between sixty-five and seventy, both hands controlling the twists and strains transmitted to the steering wheel. It was work, hot and with a high level of wind noise. Still half a tank of gas. He felt good, glancing at the rearview mirror and at the red-brown mountains to the east—they were the color of Mars—asking Rosen if he knew why they called it the Red Sea, keeping him from thinking too much.

Why?

Because, see those mountains, the color? Like dull,

dirty copper. They go all the way down into Saudi Arabia and they say their reflection on the water makes the sea look red.

Within a few miles they'd come to a stone marker and a side road—not a road; a trail—that led east, toward the mountains. It wouldn't be long. He remembered something.

"Look in the glove box," Davis said.

He'd forgotten until now Tali putting a handgun in there as they drove away from her apartment: a .22 Beretta Parabellum. Low caliber, but an effective, mean-looking gun. Rosen held it in his hands, studying it.

"It's loaded," Davis said. "Keep it on you."

The claymores were on the back seat, each wrapped in about three hundred feet of wire.

He'd need a few minutes to set the caps and attach the wires to the car battery. The Mercedes would have to hang back, cautious, suspicious, and give him time. They could do it, set up a bushwhack and invite the three guys to walk in. This was the place for it. They fought wars here, and they hadn't seen another car or truck or donkey since Mizpeh Ramon. He didn't want to miss the road marker or forget details talking to Rosen, keeping him occupied. He hoped the marker was still there. Once there had been a sign, Zohar had said, but now the sign was gone. The sign with the name of the village was gone and the people who had lived in the village were gone. Driven out by the tanks.

Rosen said he had to take a leak. Davis asked if he wanted him to stop. He thought of Raymond Garcia—

seeing him in front of the Marine House polishing his Camaro—and told Rosen to go on the floor if he had to. Rosen said no, he'd wait. He kept talking.

He said, "Listen, you know what I was? I was a Storekeeper Third. I counted skivvy shirts, for Christ's sake. The war was over before I got overseas."

"We don't have time to put you through Boot," Davis said, "but you've had all the experience you need. How long you been driving?"

"I don't know, thirty years. Longer 'n that."

"Okay, you know how to start a car. That's all you have to do. I'll throw the switch if you want," Davis said, "but then I'm not outside watching if something goes wrong."

"I'll do it," Rosen said.

"Just keep telling yourself those guys back there want to kill you," Davis said. "I'd think you'd be anxious to have it done."

"Anxious? Christ, I'm anxious, I'm scared is what I am."

"Well, I am too," Davis said. "Those guys back there—everybody's a little scared, I imagine, nervous. But what can you do? Right?"

They talked and Rosen asked about combat, what the feeling was like, people shooting at you. Scary. And about guys risking their lives. Were they crazy? You don't think, Davis said, you do it. That's what all the training was about. And medals—Rosen got on medals again. (Is that what he wanted?) What did you have to do to win different medals? Did you think at the time if it was worth it or not?

It was a situation you found yourself in, Davis said. "Over there, a Bronze Star was like a good-conduct medal. Win a Silver Star, maybe you held off twenty gooks coming through the wire with an M–16 and a bayonet. Navy Cross, you held off two hundred gooks coming through the wire with the same thing. And a Medal of Honor, you held off that many without an M–16 or a bayonet."

"Were you decorated?" Rosen asked.

"Silver Star and two Hearts."

"Really? You were wounded?"

"I got shot," Davis said.

"Jesus . . . and you got a Silver Star? What'd you do?"

The road marker was about fifty meters ahead on the left, coming up fast.

"Hang on," Davis said.

RASHAD THOUGHT it was a gust of wind blowing sand across the desert. But then Teddy Cass saw it and sat up, hunched toward the windshield.

"He turned off. You see him? That's his dust," Teddy said. "Val, is there a road here, going east?"

"Nothing," Valenzuela said.

"Maybe a kibbutz, or some kind of historic site," Teddy said.

"Nothing's supposed to be there." Valenzuela held the map up, squinting at it.

"Well, there's *some*thing," Rashad said. He could see flashes of green leading the column of dust, sun reflections on the Camaro. And beyond—something. It looked like a rock formation at first. Rashad slowed the Mercedes and turned at the stone marker, expecting a road and seeing only faint tracks through the sand and scrub ahead of the car. The dust from the Camaro was thinning, blowing away. They could see the shapes of buildings now. Inside the Mercedes, moving at about twenty-five now to avoid the rocks and depressions, they were aware of the stillness, the silence outside. There was no sign of the Camaro.

"He's making his move," Valenzuela said. His tone was like a sigh.

IT HAD BEEN a village of immigrant Jews from India, a village of stone and cement houses with flat roofs built around a square where there had been a well with a dripping faucet. Ein Kfar. The village had appeared in the sights of Israeli and Jordanian tank gunners in October, 1973, during the Yom Kippur War, and had been shelled out of existence as a place to live. Fragments of the village remained: the outline of the square, the dry faucet, walls pierced by explosives, cisterns blown out of the ground, hollow buildings with open doors, rubble in the desert sun.

A year ago Davis had passed through Ein Kfar with Raymond Garcia and Zohar, and Zohar had told them about the tank battle: how his tank had been hit by a rocket, how he had lost his gunner and loader and had been burned on his hands and face and had lain for a day in the field hospital that was set up in Ein Kfar.

Davis could still picture the village. He remembered a Coca-Cola sign lying in the rubble. He remembered thinking that Coca-Cola in Hebrew looked like Coca-Cola in English upside down.

He remembered the square—it was the same—and the narrow street to the right of the square where the sign had been. The sign was still there. And the cement walls with windows and doors blown out.

They would have to move fast now and hope that the Mercedes would hang back, not seeing the green car, and approach the village cautiously. They would have maybe five minutes.

From the square, halfway down the side street, Davis pulled the Camaro into a space between two buildings. The way ahead was clear if they had to run; they wouldn't have to back out. Okay, open the trunk. Get the shotgun first.

He said to Rosen, "Ready?"

"God," Rosen said, but he was out of the car. He walked out to the street, toward the square.

Davis pulled the Kreighoff out of the trunk, loaded both under-over barrels, and stuffed a handful of shells in the right-hand pocket of his jacket. He leaned the shotgun against the side of the Camaro.

From the back seat he got his Colt automatic first, stuck it into his pants in front; the box of cartridges went into his left-hand pocket. Then the claymore mines.

It took less than two minutes to attach the electrical

wires from the claymores to the alternator under the Camaro's hood, then unreel the wires, carrying the curved, green-painted mines one at a time out to the street, several houses down toward the square, where Rosen was piling rubble in the narrow street: old boards, hunks of concrete, pieces of furniture. Davis planted the claymores in the rubble. When he brought the third one out and buried it, he dragged the Coca-Cola sign over and laid it across the heap of debris that now blocked the street.

Rosen looked at him, tense, his eyes wide open. He took out a pack of cigarettes and got one lit. Davis adjusted his cap, looking toward the square in the sunlight. There was no sound yet, no movement.

"We're about ready," Davis said.

They walked back to the Camaro and Davis picked up the shotgun. "I'll be across the street"—he nodded—"in that window. You stand by the corner of the house. Right here. When they come, they'll see all that shit piled in the road. What're they gonna think? We're trying to delay them. Maybe we've got guns, they don't know. I imagine they'll be careful at first. But when nothing happens—they got to get out of the car to move all that stuff. When they do, when they're bending over the pile, you reach into Raymond Garcia's hot setup and turn the key on."

"You'll be right across the street," Rosen said.

Davis nodded. "I'll be right across the street. Maybe all three won't get out. Whoever's driving maybe. I'll take that one."

"You think the mines'll do it, huh?"

"They got a punch. They'll do it."

"Then what?" Rosen said.

Davis looked at him a moment. "See if they're all dead."

"Jesus," Rosen said.

The Marine touched Rosen's shoulder and walked away with the shotgun. He walked across the street. Rosen watched him. He didn't hunch his shoulders or run, he walked.

Davis looked back when he was on the other side, then stepped through a doorway, into a house with plaster ripped from the walls and only part of a roof, a house he had been in before in Phu Bai and Hue.

RASHAD PULLED closer to the buildings on the right, still in the square, and stopped. His hand dropped to the Beretta, 9mm, that was on the seat next to him. Teddy Cass's Uzi submachine gun lay across his lap, the clip sticking down between his legs. Valenzuela had taken his Uzi out of the attaché case and held it so that the barrel stub rested on the back of the front seat.

"Go on a little more," Valenzuela said. "Up to the street."

Rashad put the Mercedes in gear and eased it, creeping forward, past the building on the corner. They saw the pile of rubble halfway down the side-street.

"What's going on?" Valenzuela said. "Okay, they went down that way. What're we supposed to think about it? Does the street go somewhere else? You see any dust?"

"Looks like a road way down there," Rashad said. "They could be gone by now."

"Or they could still be here," Valenzuela said.

"Maybe that's what they want us to do," Rashad said. "Waste some time."

"Fucking Marine," Valenzuela said. "He's got no fucking business in this."

DAVIS WATCHED them advancing: the heavyset guy, Valenzuela, on this side of the street, and the thin guy with the hair on the other side, both with Uzis, banana clips, thirty rounds each, both of them staying close to the walls of the houses, coming to doorways and windows and poking the machine guns in as they took a look. The Mercedes was creeping along, staying even with them. Half a block, they'd get tired of it. They'd be anxious, realize soon they were wasting time. Clear the stuff out of the road and get moving—look for the car, find the car first, that would be the way to do it.

If he had an M–16 all three of them could be dead in the time he thought about it and pictured himself doing it. They thought they were being careful, but they didn't know shit about entering a village.

Across the street, Rosen was watching them, pressed against the wall, inching his bearded face past the corner, then pulling it back. Twice Rosen looked over his shoulder at the Camaro, making sure it was still there.

Davis held the Kreighoff cradled in his arms, his back to the front wall of the house, looking on an angle through the open window. He'd have to shoot left-handed. The shotgun had a nice balance and feel—the checkered walnut stock, the delicate, thin little gold-plated triggers. Twelve gauge: it would hold a shot pattern two fists wide from the window to the pile of rubble. Put both of them through the windshield of the Mercedes as the smoke cleared and go out with the Colt, if it was necessary to finish up.

Rosen was peeking again, holding the Beretta at his side. The rear end of the Camaro was shiny though filmed with dust. Rosen was still watching them.

They were about three houses from the rubble. The heavyset one, Valenzuela, was coming out into the street, in front of the Mercedes, saying something to the one with the hair. Now the one with the hair was coming over. Then Valenzuela motioned for the car to come on, follow them. They were walking toward the pile of rubble, tired of fooling around.

Walking into it. Davis watched them. Two houses from the rubble. He glanced over at Rosen, across the street. About thirty seconds more.

Rosen was pressed to the corner of the building.

No—he was turning away, moving quickly to the Camaro and getting in . . .

Davis couldn't believe it. Not yet! Wait!

. . . slamming the door.

Actually slamming it. Christ, he could hear it across the street. They heard it too, both of them, down the street past the pile of rubble, looking up, raising the machine guns this way.

The claymores went off as Rosen turned the ignition key—two of them did—with a hard, heavy, ear-splitting BA-WHAM-BA-WHAM, and the Coca-Cola sign and the lumber and concrete exploded in gray smoke and fragments of junk and metal, fanning out in the arc-shape of the oval claymores, blowing the shit out of the pile of rubble but missing—Davis *knew* it—the two guys flat in the street now and the black guy safe in the car. Shit. He brought up the Kreighoff and gave them both loads, knowing it was too far, knowing it was time to get the hell out—and ran across the street with the shotgun, digging the Colt out with his free hand, letting go at them, snapping shots as they got up—one of them still on his knees—firing bursts from the Uzis, trying to catch him, spray him with the dry chattering sound, taking out cement from the corner of the house as he got past it and landed hard against the trunk lid of the Camaro.

When he got around to the side, there was Rosen behind the wheel, looking up at him.

"I get 'em?"

"Shit," Davis said. "You got shit."

They drove out of there, straight out across the desert, bounding over holes and washes, tearing through the scrub, beating the hell out of Raymond Garcia's hot setup in a wide wide arc that should bring them to the highway.

"Well, for Christ sake," Rosen said. "A noise like that, Jesus, why didn't it kill them?"

Davis hung on to the wheel. He wouldn't say anything to the man for a while. He'd be looking at the rearview mirror again. Shit. He was tired of looking at the mirror, but he'd be looking at it now all the way to the Red Sea.

17

THEY SAID Teddy Cass, before he turned freelance, had done beautiful work in the precision application of explosives. He made destruction a work of art.

With Universal Demolition, Inc., Teddy had torn down at least a dozen major structures. He'd torn down, for example, the Broadmoor Hotel in Atlantic City, twelve stories, in less than twelve seconds, not even rattling the windows in a building twenty feet away—using, Teddy had once said, "a little dynamite and a lot of gravity."

The pay had been good, but it hadn't compared to what he could make working contract jobs on his own, and he'd done several for Val and Mr. Manza. (He'd gotten a grand for the first one: letting Val tie up a guy on the top floor of the Huron Hotel in Saginaw before he blew it down.) This one, five grand plus expenses. Good wages. Probably a grand or fifteen hundred more than Clarence "Rashad" Robinson was making.

But the contract hadn't said anything about taking on the fucking Marines.

Teddy told Valenzuela—in the Mercedes again going south—that it was time to renegotiate. He didn't mind discussing it in front of Rashad, because he knew Rashad would be on his side and it would be two of them Val would have to keep happy if he wanted a job done.

They were somewhere behind the green Camaro. They knew it hadn't doubled back north, they'd seen enough of its dust trail to be sure of that. But the Camaro wasn't in sight now—even with Rashad hitting ninety on clear stretches of blacktop—and they didn't know what the problems would be locating the Camaro in Eilat or at points south.

Valenzuela was not a man who became excited. He took things one at a time and looked at them.

He said, "I agree, it's different than it was on paper. We told you Ross, Rosen, never packed but was likely to now. Or he might've hired somebody who packed. But, no, we never saw something like this, a guy who carries fucking grenades in his car or whatever it was he used. So all right, you feel you're entitled to combat pay, whatever you want to call it. Let me know what you want. Harry or myself, we're not gonna argue with you. Harry wants it done, so do I."

Rashad, holding his gaze on the road and the sweep of desert, said, "Something you might consider. The man has money. He's living on something. And we know his lawyer come to give him some more. If we was to get our hands on that money and cut it up—"

Rashad said. "Hey, sight unseen, I'd go for a share, not even knowing how much we talking about."

"That's a possibility," Valenzuela said. "When you take Ross, I doubt we'll have time to ask him where his money is. But Mel, that's something else. I'm agreeable to, as you say, renegotiating. The thing is, if we keep after him we're gonna get him, I know that. We're too close to blow it now and have to start over. We're gonna agree—whatever you want and think is fair. I just don't want to stop and talk it over. The other thing—"

Valenzuela looked down at his map. "Where they going? How far? Well, they could go to Eilat and try and hide there—it looks like a pretty good-size place, a resort town, the Miami Beach of Israel—or they could keep going south, down to the southern tip of the Sinai. Then what? Go back up the other side? They keep going they'll be in Egypt. So I don't know where the fuck we're going. All I can tell you is, don't worry about the expense. Okay? Shit, we're this far. You got something else you'd rather do?"

They passed army vehicles going north and a road that pointed west, to the Timna Mining Company. About three miles from Eilat, they approached a security checkpoint: a shed at the side of the road with yellow markings and two Israeli men in khaki clothes—though not army uniforms—with submachine guns slung over their shoulders.

Rashad said, "Uh-oh."

Teddy Cass pushed his Uzi under the front seat. Valenzuela's lay across his legs, beneath the open map of Israel. He put his hand on the weapon as the car crept up to the two security men studying them, one with his hand raised. The hand moved then, waving them past. Rashad began to accelerate. Valenzuela said, "No, hold on. Stop."

Rashad braked. One of the security men walked over to the open window on Teddy's side. "Ask him about a green car," Valenzuela said.

"Yeah, say," Teddy said to the security man, who was middle-aged and weathered and had probably been in several wars, "did a green American car go by here a few minutes ago? Some friends of ours, we're supposed to meet them down here."

The security man was nodding, saying yes and waving his arm, yes, it went by.

"Thank him," Valenzuela said.

They came to Eilat feeling better about their prospects—to the desert town on the side of a hill, a boom town of new houses and young trees and children—young people everywhere—the town spreading up the hill from the gulf, down the south coast into the Sinai, with its airport right in the middle.

Valenzuela studied his map and made a plan.

They dropped Rashad off at the airport to wait there, which was fine with him, get out of the car for a while. Teddy slid behind the wheel and they circled around the airport to drive through the parking lots of the half dozen hotels lining the curve of the gulf that was called the North Beach. No green Camaro. Rosen and the Marine couldn't have taken the road east, because it didn't go anywhere. The road stopped at the

border, at Aqaba, and you couldn't get into Jordan
from Israel without a visa. You couldn't sneak in far-
ther north because of the mine fields. There was nothing west but desert and mountains all the way to Suez.

So they drove south, winding along the shore of the
gulf, past the port facilities and oil storage tanks, slowing down at a couple of motels, stopping at the
Laromme to inspect the parking area, and then going
on another five or six miles, between the mountains
and the coral beaches on the edge of the sea—to another security checkpoint.

Valenzuela, in the front seat now, said, "You
wouldn't happen to've seen a bright green American
car go by here, would you? With a white stripe?" A
Z–28 Camaro? the security man with the M–16 asked.
"Yeah, that's the one," Valenzuela said. No, the security man said, he had seen that car one time and heard
its engine and liked it very much, the sound, *rrrrrrruuu-
uum,* but he had not seen it today. He wanted to know
if the owner was a friend of theirs and how many liters
the engine was and if the owner wanted to sell it.
Christ, discussing a hot rod, with the mountains of
Jordan and Saudi Arabia over there across the gulf and
a Bedouin going by on a camel.

It was worth it. Rosen and the Marine were in Eilat.

"Now what?" Teddy said.

"We'll check with Clarence," Valenzuela said. He
was thinking as he spoke. "We got to station ourselves
somewhere, different places, but so we can get a-hold
of each other quick. You know what I mean? Say
Clarence stays at the airport. You're in town, or I'm in

town. The other one drives around. You go to the checkpoints a few times a day, shoot the shit with the guy about cars, and find out if a green one happened to go by lately. That's what we do, keep looking, ask around for our friends. Hey, you know a guy who drives a green Camaro? Pretty soon one of them's gonna go to the store for a six-pack. It's a matter of time," Valenzuela said, nodding, thinking about it. "That's all it is. Time."

18

OFF THE SOUTH BEACH ROAD, a few miles from the Hotel Laromme, there was a place called Wadi Shlomo where pilgrim caravans from North Africa, on their way to Mecca, would come down out of the high desert to the sea.

Now, a trail followed the wadi, the dry wash, twin ruts that twisted through the hardpack for several miles—a mystery trail that offered little hope of leading anywhere—before coming within sight of the doctor's residence.

There. A whitewashed adobe, a desert home with a low, flat roof. Not bad in Tucumcari, New Mexico; a dazzler in the Sinai, sitting there with its patio and carport, a bird feeder on a pole, windmill and stock tank in back, the house edged with scrub trees and coarse grass, a low stone fence across the front of the property with a wooden gate that was open.

"They're not home," Rosen said. "Both cars are gone."

Coming through the gate, they could see that the carport was empty. Davis drove slowly, looking around, staying in the ruts that curved up to the house.

"Well, I guess it doesn't matter," Rosen said. "There's supposed to be a key in the birdhouse. He's something; he goes off into the desert to take care of the Bedouins, he locks the house and tells everybody where the key is. Says in case he and Fay are gone, go in and have a drink, make yourself at home. Reginald drinks some kind of Arab piss, raki or arak or something. It's awful. But I know Fay keeps a bottle of Johnny Walker Red in the cupboard over the sink."

Rosen was talkative again, the nervous excitement gone out of him, high now on a feeling of relief. From Ein Kfar to Eilat he had kept shaking his head and saying shit no, hey, that kind of business was way way out of his line. He didn't have the background to stand there and watch them and wait for just the right moment. Christ, those guys had ma*chine* guns. He could still hear it, the gunfire. He hadn't thought it would be that loud or affect him the way it had. He was sorry, he wasn't making any excuses, it just wasn't his line. Christ, all the time in the Navy during the Great War, Storekeeper Third, he hadn't fired a gun in anger, shit, he'd hardly even fired one at all except in boot camp, and then the noise, the racket inside the place on the firing range with the oh-threes going off, drove him nuts. Shit, he didn't even qualify with the oh-three.

Now he felt safe and could relax and tell Davis

about the Bedouin doctor who lived in Eilat and de-
voted his practice to the Sinai desert Arabs, going out
in his Land Rover to visit the trailer clinics he had established during the past twenty years. Reginald
Morris and his wife Fay. Reginald very British and
proper in his blazer and rep tie, with a sense of humor
as dry as his desert, a leftover colonial from the time of
the raj, his own man, who grumbled about ineffective
governments and saved lives. Fay, Rosen said, was sort
of a nutty lady. He loved her English accent. She chat-
tered, and she could carry an evening all by herself and
keep you smiling. She was comfortable while Reginald
pretended to be gruff. She accepted the desert in the
fashion of a colonial wife, and when she felt a little
down or bored or lonely, she could always take a pull
on the Johnny Walker Red above the sink. Rosen had
felt good here, in their company. It was another reason
he felt safe now—once they'd found a ladder to get the
key out of the birdhouse and covered the Camaro, in
the carport, with a canvas tarp.

There was anything they wanted to drink, except
bourbon; even cold beer in the humming refrigerator.
No phone; but electricity, hot water, and a bathtub.

Davis said he'd have a beer and walked through the
rooms looking out the windows at the stone fence and
at the scrub growth and desert on four sides.

The patio, with its umbrella table and old-fashioned
striped canvas beach chairs, was on the left side of the
house looking out. Coming in through the sliding glass
doors, the change was abrupt: from desert living to
country English, a room full of heavy pieces—deep

chairs and a sofa slipcovered in floral designs, dark wood tables, and secretary with china figurines on the shelves.

There was a low roof or ramada that ran along the front of the house to the carport on the other side. The two bedrooms and bath were on that side of the house. The kitchen extended across the back, with a heavy oak table separating it from the living room.

The living room wasn't the place to be if they came from the patio side. The glass doors offered no protection. Windows filled the front wall. They opened out and gave a view of the yard and the stone fence about fifty meters away. One of them would have to be here, to watch the front and the patio side of the house. The other one would have to be in the back bedroom, to watch the side, past the carport, and the whole back-yard area. It wasn't a good place to defend.

If they came, he'd have to get Rosen out of here and go up into the rocks, find some high ground. He'd have to take a look after a while. Rosen, sipping his Scotch now, saying, "Ahhhh," would argue and not want to go. They needed more guns.

"Here are some pictures of them"—Rosen standing by a wall of photographs in the living room—"a good one of Fay. Here's Reginald in a Bedouin outfit. He's always Reginald, never Reg or Reggie. Very formal guy on the surface."

"Does he hunt?" Davis said.

"You mean go hunting?"

"Does he have any guns."

"Well, I don't know if we should nose around in their personal things. Having a drink, well, he said to."

"Let's look," Davis said.

He found a Mauser safari rifle, 30–06, five-shot, in the front closet, oiled, in perfect condition.

Rosen came out of the back bedroom with a heavy revolver that had "Enfield Mark VI" stamped on the side plate. It was at least seventy-five years old, but it was loaded. He made another drink and watched Davis assembling the guns on the oak table—three handguns now, the shotgun and a good rifle, with boxes of ammo—and then slipping on his shoulder rig and putting the Colt automatic in the holster.

Rosen said, "Come on, sit down and rest awhile. They're not gonna find us."

"Maybe not today," Davis said.

"Fine, then we'll worry about it tomorrow," Rosen said. "I'll tell you, the worst thing in any situation is not knowing what you're gonna do. But once you make the decision, the hard part's over. All you have to do then is do it. I'm not gonna fight those guys. I've got no business even thinking about it. So I'm getting out. Fuck the money. I'll call Mel, have him deliver it some other time. I'm not gonna worry about that now. All I want to do is get my passport and get out of the country."

Davis said, "That's all, huh?"

"I know, it's gonna take some juking around," Rosen said. "But look, Edie's at the Laromme—they flew in, she got there even before we got here. The hotel's right down the beach. Cut across the desert, you could probably walk it in a couple of hours."

"If you don't get lost," Davis said.

"I'm saying it's a possibility. And Tali'll be here tomorrow with the car."

"Probably tomorrow."

"A day or two doesn't matter now. I fly out of here or drive up to Ben Gurion and get the first plane to Athens, either way. I mean when we see it's clear, and that's where we—or I should say *I*—will have to do some finessing around first, I know that. But I'm going. You guys with the firearms, man, that's way out of my line. I'm not saying I haven't *seen* any of it before, don't get me wrong." Rosen paused and took a drink of Scotch.

"I understand what you mean," Davis said. "We tried something and it didn't work. Only it isn't a question now of you saying okay, fine, let's forget about it and go home."

Rosen wasn't listening to him.

"I'll tell you something," Rosen said. "The way I started out, I could've easily been on the other side of the fence, I mean working for somebody like Harry Manza. Shit, I could've *been* Harry Manza. Years ago, the things I was into—but on the fringe, not all the way. I worked for a guy in the loan-shark business. I was his bookkeeper. I worked for a guy in the protective insurance business—listen, that hotel fire that got my picture in the paper. You think it *caught* fire? That was the protection business. Even said it in the papers. That's the kind of shit they pull if you don't want to sign up and make your payments. They burn down the whole fucking hotel. I worked in a guy's office who was in that business. I was just twenty-three years old. I was with the Teamsters—that's a long story, I won't go into it, but I was in Jimmy Hoffa's Local two-nine-nine in Detroit, back in the Fifties, and you didn't have to go to the movies if you wanted to see some action. I've had some situations since that time where you're dealing with people . . . well, you know, I told you about some of that. You get the Justice Department on you, get squeezed between the bad guys and the fucking good guys, the government lawyers, who don't give a rat's ass what happens to you, leave you standing there with your yang hanging out. I know about dealing with all kinds of people. I know what those guys eat for breakfast, and I also know when to pull my head in to keep it from getting shot off. If it was a deal, we were talking to those guys, shit, I could sell them anything. How about some development land out in a fucking mine field between Israel and Jordan? They'd buy it. But if I can't get close enough to talk and know they're gonna listen, then, man, I walk away."

"I'm not arguing with you," Davis said.

"What I am, what you see, is a retired businessman," Rosen said. "I'm getting a little too old for this kind of bullshit. Listen, I'll admit it."

"I don't see that age has anything to do with it," Davis said, "if they come to kill you."

Rosen hesitated a moment. "You believe in God?"

Then Davis hesitated. "Yeah, I guess so."

"Well, I'll have to tell you what I think about the Will of God," Rosen said. "You might be interested. Mainly it's accepting things that happen to you. But it doesn't mean standing there when you can move out of the way. I'm too old to be playing guns," Rosen said. "But I'm not too old to run like a sonofabitch."

19

AT DUSK, Davis took the Kreighoff and went on a recon, down the road that followed the wadi, for almost a mile, then came back and circled the perimeter of Dr. Morris' house in the gray desert silence. He couldn't imagine people walking across this land, coming all the way from Egypt and the Suez. He couldn't imagine the Bedouins living out there. The first Bedouin he had ever seen—on the trip with Zohar and Raymond Garcia, west of here at Um Sidra, the Wadi of Inscriptions—was a boy of about fourteen; he'd worn a yellow sport shirt and black pointed shoes with thin soles and had seemed to appear out of nowhere with a guest register under his arm, asking for their signatures. Visitors, centuries before, had carved their names in the rocks of Um Sidra; now they signed a guest book. Zohar had asked the boy in Arabic where he lived. He'd pointed off somewhere at the empty desert. Zohar had asked him where he got water and he'd pointed in another direction. Davis thought of the tourists who came to the desert in their hiking boots and safari outfits, and the guidebook warnings to keep your head covered in the sun; and then he thought of the Bedouin boy in his yellow shirt and pointy shoes and no hat.

Maybe, as Rosen said, you could walk to the Laromme from here, approach the hotel from the desert. That would be the way to do it. They couldn't drive the Camaro. It would be better, too, if he went alone and Rosen stayed at the house. He'd wait for Tali and bring her back here with Rosen's clothes and passport. Maybe drive him down to Sharm el Sheikh. Fly out from there.

He didn't see any high ground or good protection within a mile of the house. But if they came during the night it would be all right. He could slip out of the house at night and if he located them he could do some mean and dirty things.

"ON THAT KIND of patrol," Davis said, "we'd be dropped in, all camied up, no helmets, equipment taped. We didn't even talk out loud. At night we'd sleep, everybody holding hands, with two guys awake, and if they heard something we'd give each other hand signals. We never dug in or left any sign we'd been there. The time I got the Star we were in there watching traffic on a supply trail and it seemed like a whole battalion of NVA got on us the first night."

"What's NVA?" Rosen said.

"North Vietnamese Army. The regulars, not the VCs."

There were shadows outside on the patio, in a haze of moonlight; the living room was dark where they sat in flowered easy chairs: Rosen with a Scotch, Davis with a can of beer and the Kreighoff next to his chair.

"See, sometimes we'd go in, we'd put up posters that said, 'The First Recon Marines are in your area. Drop your fucking weapons and surrender.' But this one was a sneak-and-peek mission and I was the patrol leader."

"How many men?"

"Twelve that time. We lost four. What we'd do, we'd radio our position before we settled in for the night, give the artillery four coordinates—what was called a killing cross—with us in the middle. We'd key the hand set. Then later on, when the NVA got on us, we'd give our signal, like"—almost whispering then—"'Magic Pie Two, this is Swift Scout,' then click twice and they'd know we needed artillery cover."

"What happens if they're off a little? The artillery," Rosen said.

"Yeah, some fuck-ups smoking dope lay it on you by mistake," Davis said. "You get fucking killed is what happens. That time on the supply trail the cover was fine, but there were too many of them. They kept trying to run over us, and our heavy stuff, our M–60 and our grenade launchers, were out, so we called back to let up on one coordinate and we slipped out that way and met our extract. That's the helicopter that pulls you out. I mean it *yanks* you out. They drop a cable and you're wearing like a parachute harness with a ring you snap on the cable and it jerks you out of there with everybody on the line banging into each other. But you're so glad to get out you don't care."

"What'd you get the Silver Star for?" Rosen said.

"For that. I was the patrol leader," Davis said. "We killed a bunch of the NVA, held them off, and I picked up an NVA field officer, brought him along. The guy was hanging on to me, he had a death grip around my neck all the time during the extract, flying out of there. But you know what the worst part of it was?"

"What?" Rosen said.

"The guy's breath. All the time he's hanging on me, strangling me to death, he's breathing in my face with a breath like he'd been eating fucking garbage and hadn't brushed his teeth in five months."

"I can't imagine living like that," Rosen said, "doing it every day."

"That time we did a job, I guess," Davis said. "We brought the NVA officer out and we brought out our dead. That was something you could count on. We always brought out our dead."

"You said you were wounded, got a couple of Purple Hearts," Rosen said. "Was one of them on that patrol?"

"No, it was another time, an emergency extract," Davis said. "This Medevac landed to pick up our wounded and I ran out with a guy over my shoulder. I got him inside all right, I looked down, there was all this blood pouring out of my leg. I didn't feel anything at the time or hear anything because of the rotors, all the fucking noise they were making. As the Medevac was rising up, I banged on the door and yelled at them, "Hey, shit, I'm wounded too! Open up!" Davis shook his head, thinking about it, and had a sip of beer.

"What was the other time?" Rosen said.

"It was practically the same time. We got up in the air and the fucking helicopter was shot down. I had my feet caught in something and when we hit I tore the tendons in the backs of my legs. That was my second Heart in about five minutes."

"But you got out."

"I'm here," Davis said.

"And you're worried about what you're gonna do. I mean when you're discharged," Rosen said. "I don't understand that. All you've been through, situations you've handled, what're you worried about?"

"I told you. I don't have a trade. My military occupational specialty is infantry, and I don't think there's much call for infantrymen in civilian life."

"Learning a trade, doing one thing the rest of your life, that's for clucks without imagination," Rosen said. "You don't, in the business world, you don't prepare yourself for a certain job and that's it, like a book-keeper, a tax accountant. You hire those people. What you do, you keep your eyes open, you use a little imagination seeing how you can fit into a situation or how you can bend the situation around so it fits you. What did I know about real estate and the mortgage business? Nothing. But I saw an opportunity, a chance to get in, talk to the right people and convince them they should be doing business with me."

"Okay," Davis said. "But I'm not worth a shit at talking to people. They'd see right away I didn't know what I was talking about. I mean if I tried to fake it, tell them I'm some kind of an expert."

"No, they wouldn't," Rosen said. "It's how you do it, your tone. They're busy thinking about themselves, what hotshots they are. They're thinking what they're gonna say to impress you. If you start right off, they see you've got confidence, you look right at them, you compliment them, bullshit them a little, they think ah, he's got good judgment, he must know what he's doing. That's all. Don't be afraid of people—Christ, I'm telling you not to be afraid. I mean in a business situation. Don't let people scare you; because nine times out of ten they don't know any more than you do. Or even less. They got there pushing and shoving, acting, conning, bullshitting. If they had to get by on basic intelligence alone—most of the people I've done business with—they'd be on the street selling Good Humors and probably fucking up the change. . . . How old are you?"

"Thirty-four," Davis said.

"I didn't get into the mortgage business till I was thirty-eight. No, thirty-nine. I didn't even know there was such a thing—lining up a shitload of mortgages and selling them to banks. A hundred million dollars worth of paper at one percent. What's that?"

"A million dollars," Davis said.

"You bet it is. A year," Rosen said. "With not an awful lot of overhead, either. Don't worry about the type of business, it's all pretty much the same. Take your time, talk to people, decide what you'd like to do, then start doing it. What I always say is, making the decision's the hard part. All this time, I mean for three years, I've been thinking I want to go home, back to the States. Then something like this happens, I have to look at my life closely again and make a decision. Why do I want to go home? Or, do I really want to go home? No, it turns out, after I analyze it, I'm happier here than I've ever been in my life. What do I want to go home for? . . . You like it here, don't you?"

"Yeah, it's all right. I guess I've had a pretty good time," Davis said.

"Palling around with Kissinger at the King David Hotel, I guess you have," Rosen said. "That reminds me, you never said who it was let the fart that time. Do you know?"

"It was me," Davis said.

"People look at you?"

"A few. There wasn't anything I could do about it, so I didn't do anything. I stood there and looked back at them."

Rosen liked that. He sat up in his chair and turned to Davis. "See? What do you mean you can't handle a situation with people? That's the whole idea, be natural, be yourself, you can't miss. Your only problem, as I see it, is making the initial decision. That's why you're here. You know that?"

"That's why I'm where? You mean sitting here?"

"Right. You're afraid to make the decision to go home."

"I'm going home," Davis said. "I just don't know what I'm gonna do."

"Yeah, but this is like delaying it. Also it's a confidence builder, it's something you know how to handle. I couldn't figure it out at first. Why you'd want to risk your neck. What're you getting out of it? You haven't said anything about money. Now I see why you got involved. You're putting off making a decision. You're sticking to what you know as long as you can."

"That's what I'm doing, huh?"

"Take my word," Rosen said. "Also believe me when I say you've got nothing to worry about dealing with people. Forget what I said about bullshitting anybody. In your case, look right at them and play it straight and you'll win. You've got a nice natural style."

THE SECURITY MAN with the green baseball cap and the submachine gun came up to Rashad the next morning at about eight-thirty—after he'd spent the night in the airport—and asked him what he was doing here.

Rashad said yeah, he was supposed to meet a friend coming in from Ben Gurion, was supposed to be *yes*-terday, but shit, he didn't know when his friend was gonna get here now. He just had to wait.

He also had to show another security man—downstairs in one of the private security booths—his passport and empty his pockets and explain again no, he wasn't an Arab, man, he was a Muslim, born in Dalton,

Georgia, lived in Detroit, and had never been to any Arab country in his life.

They still watched him. He'd walk over to the Arkia counter and look at the TV screen of arrivals and departures—almost every hour of the day between here and Ben Gurion—and then walk over to the lunch counter and have a cup of coffee and go look out the window or stand by the stairs going down to the lower level and look in the big mirror mounted on the landing that showed the security booths and the departure waiting area.

The arrivals didn't come in through the terminal. They'd get off the plane, pick up their luggage from the train of baggage carts, and walk through the gate to the street. At ten o'clock, outside for some fresh air, watching a group of passengers that had just gotten off a plane, Rashad saw a familiar face.

A woman. A nicely dressed woman with a group of women laughing and carrying on, acting like little girls. Americans. Maybe from the Hilton. Or the Pal. He might've seen her in the lobby one time.

Staring at the woman he made himself remember. It wasn't in Tel Aviv, it was Jerusalem. And not *in* a hotel, but coming out. With the man, Mr. Rosen. Walking to his car.

All the women were crowded around the entrance of a red-and-white Egged Tour bus while their luggage was being loaded on. Rashad waited. He was the last one to step aboard, jumping in just as the door was about to snap closed. When the driver looked at him funny, Rashad handed him a ten-pound note.

"You going to the hotel, aren't you?"

The driver nodded.

"I just want a lift, man. I'll stand right here out of the way."

That was how Rashad got to the Laromme on the south beach road and how he came to be hanging around the lobby, watching the woman friend of Mr. Rosen's, when another friend of Mr. Rosen's, the Israeli chick with the nice ass, Tali, walked up to the woman and started talking to her.

On the phone a few minutes later, when he heard Valenzuela's voice, Rashad said, "You gonna like what I got to tell you."

20

WHAT GENE VALENZUELA liked was the view of all the cement work going on.

At half past ten, when the phone rang in the café, Valenzuela was on an upper-level terrace not more than a half mile from Rashad. The terrace, which ran along in front of the café in a clean new complex of mini-mall shops and fast-food places, got the sun directly and was hot at midmorning, but it gave Valenzuela a treeless view of everything. Directly below him, the road came curving in from the south beach and fingered out in three directions: across open, undeveloped land to the North Beach hotels; to the airport; and up the hill to town.

The cement work was done in a hurry; it didn't have a nice finished look. But it was new and clean. He'd think about the old, gray-peeling cement at Lewisburg (with the highest homicide rate of any federal prison), hard motherfuckers fighting over the queens. He'd watch the Israeli girls walk by in their jeans with their Jewish asses. There was a crowd of young stuff here and enough cement work—a guy with half a dozen transit-mixers could make enough to retire in three years.

When the phone rang in the café he thought of his wife and pictured her talking on the phone in her smart-ass voice to her mother—"*I* don't know where he is, the sonofabitch. Who knows? He never tells me where he goes and I personally don't care."

She'd never find him, either. She'd never even heard of Eilat. Shit, who had? He'd bet Harry Manza had never heard of it. But if it was a money-maker, it wouldn't matter to Harry where it was. Get some development capital from him. Cash. Sneak it into the country. Nothing signed with him, no written agreements. Harry had to die sometime. Valenzuela saw himself sitting here with a growing business. Let his wife keep wondering where he was. Let her bitch and never have to listen to her again.

On the phone, talking to Rashad, he said, "Okay, stay there. Teddy's due to call or come by here in about . . . fifteen, twenty minutes. We'll meet you outside the hotel."

"ISRAELI GIRLS are funny," Davis was saying to Rosen at ten that morning, in the kitchen having coffee. "Or maybe all girls are funny, I mean different, and I don't know how to read them."

"It's a knack," Rosen said. "First you've got to never be awed. Though you're polite, of course."

"This girl I picked up one time at the Shalom Tower," Davis said. "We're getting along fine, having a coffee. She says she's meeting her girlfriend from England at the El Al terminal. So we pick her up, a really good-looking girl with the long blonde hair and the English accent and all, and we go to the Israeli girl's apartment. She says she's got a bottle of wine there and some hash. So I'm thinking fine, one girl or the other, I can't miss. We get to the apartment, the Israeli girl's *hus*band's there. Listen to this. I end up talking to the husband about the West Bank situation while the two broads are off in the bedroom making out."

He was never sure Rosen listened, because Rosen seldom commented. He would start talking right away, saying something that didn't always follow.

"I learned a long time ago," Rosen said, "the most overrated thing in the world—you know what it is?"

"What?"

"Teenage pussy. That young stuff, you say, oh man—they don't even know half the time what to do with it. They're thinking about their hair. Their minds jump around too much. From my experience—you don't have to believe this, but it's true—the best is a younger middle-aged woman recently divorced or widowed. By recently I mean within a couple of years. I'll qualify that still further. Naturally she's got to be good-looking and you don't want a real fat one or one that wears a lot of makeup to hide her age and looks great only in the Hilton lounge, but after—you know what I mean. It's true. Good-looking, stylish, middle-aged broads with some background, you know, somebody you can talk to. Otherwise, if all you want's a jump, get a whore, it's cheaper. No, but you see stylish tourist ladies—you see them all the time at the King David, the Hilton, the International. Well, the International, I'm not so sure. But which ones do you think'd be better in bed, the tourist ladies that stay at the King David or the ones that stay at the Hilton? You've been to the Hilton, haven't you? In Jerusalem?"

"Yeah, I've been there."

"And you know what the King David looks like."

"Sure."

"Okay, which you think would be better?"

"What's the difference?" Davis said.

"I'll tell you," Rosen said, in the kitchen of the desert house, seated at the table, looking up at Davis standing by the sink. "The Hilton lady, usually her clothes are more expensive. She spends a little more on herself, her hair, and she's more likely to wear designer labels. The King David lady is a little plainer on the average, though in very good taste. She's quieter and not as easy to meet. But once you get next to her—you know what I mean—the King David lady is better in bed. You know why?"

"Why?"

"Because usually it's been a longer time since she's had it. She's more grateful and, hence, she gives more of herself."

"That's interesting," Davis said.

"It's a fact, based on research," Rosen said. "Eight out of ten divorced wives of doctors and orthodontists who stay at the King David are better in bed. Make it sound more scientific."

Davis put his cup in the sink. His hand came up and touched the Colt holstered beneath his jacket.

"Well, listen, I'd like to stay and chat with you some more, but I think I better get going."

"You come back," Rosen said, "bring me some Winstons. Hey . . . and my passport."

RASHAD HAD TO LOOK for the gray Mercedes; first, standing in the shade of the canopy over the entrance, then seeing he'd have to walk through the aisles of cars. He found it parked down near the end of a row. The engine was running and the air-conditioning was on. Rashad stooped at the window on Teddy's side, looking past Teddy at Valenzuela.

"You see him go in? The Marine?"

"He's in there?" Valenzuela straightened.

"It was good I saw him first. I'm standing in the lobby. I turn around, he's walking over to the desk."

"Yeah? What'd he do?"

"He got in a elevator, went upstairs."

"How long ago was that?"

"Five minutes," Rashad said. "I just seen him. I couldn't believe it, I turn around, there he is with his cap on."

"But no sign of Rosen, uh?"

"No, I looked around some."

"How about the girl, Tali?"

"She went up before, with the woman."

Valenzuela nodded. "Then the Marine comes and he goes up. Like they have it arranged." Valenzuela was silent a moment. "You didn't see the girl at the airport. Just the woman."

"That's right," Rashad said.

"So she got a ride or she drove his car. We'll look around for it." Valenzuela was silent again. He shrugged. "Then see what happens."

EDIE, SITTING ON THE BED, told them the story of how the charter flight had been cancelled yesterday after they'd waited around the airport for hours, of then going back to the Hilton on the tour bus, another hour, and of waiting again while the baggage was unloaded and carried up to the room, of then not having anything to do yesterday afternoon. . . .

Tali sat there patiently. Davis sat there thinking, Come on, get to the end!

. . . Then this morning doing it all over again, going out to the airport at seven, two hours earlier, waiting some more, going through security, and the charter finally leaving at ten.

Why is it so important to her? Davis was thinking.

Why didn't she ask about Rosen? She had asked, yes, how he was. But why wouldn't he be the only thing on her mind? Tali must have talked to her yesterday and explained a little of the situation. Why wasn't she concerned about him? No, people had their own concerns—cancelled flights—that were just as important.

He said, "You have his passport?"

"I thought I was going to see him," Edie said, surprised now after all that.

"In case he doesn't get by this way," Davis said. "I don't know what his plans are."

"Well, if that's the way he wants to be," Edie said. "If he wants to keep on being the mystery man . . ."

Davis looked at Tali as the woman went over to her suitcase and pulled out Rosen's safari jacket. Tali glanced at him, but her expression told him nothing.

"Tell him we're leaving here tomorrow afternoon at five-thirty," Edie said. "If he wants to call me, I think it would be nice."

"There's no phone where he is," Davis said. "Maybe you don't understand. He's in a lot of trouble."

Edie came over to hand him the jacket. "Maybe I don't understand," she said. "According to Tali, some crazy people are trying to kill him. But I know he tends to be a little dramatic. The mysterious American living in the Middle East. Am I supposed to believe he's a spy, something like that? I'll say one thing, he's entertaining. But I'm afraid I don't have enough motivation or incentive to wait around while Al Rosen plays his games, or whatever he's doing. If he wants to see me today or tomorrow, fine. If he doesn't, well . . . his passport and sunglasses are in the pocket."

"I'll tell him," Davis said.

TALI BROUGHT the black Mercedes up to the front entrance and when Davis got in and they drove off, turning south, she continued to tell him about the woman, saying she thought the woman had no feeling or the woman had something else on her mind.

"She was very nervous yesterday," Tali said, "when I drove her to her hotel. Then I didn't see her again until this morning."

"How about Mati?" Davis said. Find that out first.

"He went back to Tel Aviv."

"You're sure?"

"Yes, I drove him to the highway to hitchhike. The woman . . . I thought she was worried about Mr. Rosen, but now I think she believes I was telling her a story. Something Mr. Rosen thought of to kid her with."

"That's something he can worry about," Davis said, "if he wants to." Davis was half turned on the seat, watching the road through the rear window.

"Yes, if he wants to," Tali said. "But I think she's too old for him."

"He's older than she is."

"He's not. Mr. Rosen is forty. He told me. That woman is at least forty-five. He'll still be young when she's old."

Davis had the jacket on his lap, Rosen's passport in the pocket.

Forget it. People lived in their own world and believed what they wanted to believe. They worried about the wrong things. Little pissy things with big problems staring at them. Tali was doing it. She believed in Rosen. She honored him. She was probably in love with the old bullshitter and didn't even know it.

"Have you been to the doctor's house?"

"Yes, once with Mr. Rosen."

"You travel with him?"

"Sometimes I do."

"His idea is to leave Israel for a while and then come back."

"Not go to the States?"

"No."

"He talked about that when I saw him last time in Netanya," Tali said. "About going home, if he could do it."

"He's decided he likes it here," Davis said.

"Good. I know, the time I'm with him, he can be very happy."

"He thinks they'll get tired of looking for him after a while."

"Yes, why not? If they see it's so very hard to catch him, then they stop and say oh well, never mind."

"You and Rosen," Davis said, "you live in a dream world. He's got a friend, or somebody he knows, guy left home, ran out on his wife and kids and owed people a lot of money. He said for ten years this guy hid out, changed his name, moved around. And you know what?—this is what Rosen says—nobody was looking for him. They were glad he was gone. That's the way Rosen thinks it'll be with him."

"I believe it," Tali said.

"Well, if nobody's interested in him, how come they're here?"

"Because of his picture. But that was an accident,"

Tali said. "He can be careful; it won't happen to him again."

"We've got to get him out of here first," Davis said. "I was thinking, drive him down to Sharm el Sheikh and fly Arkia out of there. Maybe go to Tiberias, some place like that."

"Of course, all the places he can go, he would never be catched." She shrugged, cocking her head to one side. "Then they get tired and go home. I'm not worry about that part. If he agrees it would be easy."

"What part are you worrying about?" Davis said.

"You." Tali glanced at him and brought her gaze back to the road. "I'm afraid you'll talk to him about fighting a war with them."

"He can do what he wants," Davis said. "I'm not in this anymore. . . . Here's where you turn."

THE SECURITY MAN at the south beach checkpoint came over to the car smiling, shaking his head at his friend Teddy Cass. "No, he wasn't by here this morning. I know that car. It's a very good car, the green one, but I still don't see it."

When they had turned around and were heading north again, Teddy said, "Between here and the hotel. That's only about a five-mile stretch. What'd we pass?"

"There was one road," Valenzuela said. "The only one I saw."

"Where?"

"You'll see it."

There was no sign at Wadi Shlomo, only the indication of a road: the two ruts in the hardpack that followed the dry creek bed up into the desert. Rashad got out with an Uzi and ran ahead of the car, scouting each bend and rise, then waving the gray Mercedes to come on. It was slow. Rashad was cautious, but he was also eager and knew it wouldn't be long.

Teddy Cass and Valenzuela held on through the creeping, jolting ride, staring at the windshield. They were eager, too, but also patient, waiting for the sign from Rashad. When he was out of sight, beyond a bend and a stand of scrub trees, and was gone this time for ten going on fifteen minutes, they sat listening to the hum of the air-conditioning unit, the sun glaring hot on the windshield, and neither of them spoke.

Then Rashad was coming back, approaching from the sandy creek bed, slipping, skinning his knee as he came up the bank, but smiling.

21

TALI SMILED, happy and relieved, as Rosen hugged her and kissed her on the cheek. He took the short-sleeved safari jacket from the Marine, put it on, buttoning one button, set his shoulders and patted the pockets as they walked past the front of the house to the patio.

"I'm home," Rosen said. "I put this on I can do anything. Tali, you're the cutest little broad in Israel and I love you. What'd you do with Edie? You talk to her?"

Davis saw Tali's expression change, the light go out of her eyes.

"She's waiting for you at the Laromme."

"She's not exactly waiting," the Marine said. "She told us you could call her if you wanted." He saw Rosen's frown. "She thinks you're pulling her chain and she's getting tired of waiting for you."

"*Wait*ing for me. She's running all over Israel with my passport. All she had to do was leave it somewhere. She said that? She's tired of waiting?"

"I don't think she understands it," Tali said.

A blue plastic pitcher and four glasses were on the patio table, beneath the umbrella. Rosen put his hand in the pitcher and stirred with one finger. They could hear the ice tinkle, the sound of something cold in the desert sun. The Marine stopped at the edge of the patio and looked back across the yard to the Mercedes in the drive and, past it, to the opening in the stone fence. In a few minutes he'd bring the car up closer to the house. Pull up behind the Camaro and maybe turn it around, pointing at the road.

"Some broads, I'm telling you," Rosen said. "They don't go one step out of their way if it's inconvenient. Okay, if I don't see her—it looks like I won't have time anyway, if we're going to Sharm el Sheikh."

Davis came over. "Why don't you take Tali with you? Have somebody to keep you company." Glancing at her. "I don't think Tali'd mind resting awhile, after all the running around she's been doing for you. But let's go inside and talk about it."

When Rosen looked at her, Tali gave her little shrug and said, "It would be fine. Whatever you want me to do."

"I *was* thinking about it," Rosen said. "I'm gonna need a cover, and I'm gonna need somebody to make contact, call my company, tell them to mail a certified check—quit screwing around with the cash idea, take the bank exchange. Listen." He turned to Davis then. "I'm gonna take care of you, too, and I don't want to hear anything about what Mel gave you. Okay?"

"I thought we were friends," Davis said.

"Of course we're friends."

"I mean I didn't sign on for pay."

"I know you didn't. But you've got a funny idea about accepting money I want to help you change. It's nice to stand up and be independent, but you can't be selfish about it. You've got to give me a chance to show off, too, and I do it with money. Okay, we're gonna make some plans. First, though"—he raised the pitcher and began pouring—"we'll have a vodka and orange juice in honor, in recognition, of my two best friends saving my ass."

He was saying, okay? Handing a glass to Tali. Saying, if you need another excuse, think of one, but we're gonna have a drink. Coming over to hand a glass to Davis . . .

Davis saw the blood coming through the breast pocket of the safari jacket, the red popping out and sounds, a grunt from Rosen, the wind knocked out of him, dropping the plastic glass. He heard the grunt and the sound of automatic weapons in the desert and the sound of the glass patio doors shattering with the continuing hard, thin chattering sound of the automatic weapons and Tali's scream, Tali holding Rosen on his feet. Davis thought she had been hit as he grabbed Rosen around the body, tight to his own body, and got him inside, into the near corner against the stucco wall, and eased him down gently. Tali was next to him, on her knees, moaning something in Hebrew, staring at Rosen.

Davis brought the Colt automatic out of its holster and began firing past the ragged edge of the glass door into the desert, making out the figures now lying in the scrub, two of them, as they continued to fire into the room, riddling the figurines in the secretary and the glass in the framed photographs of the Bedouin doctor and his wife, wiping them from the wall. There was a pause, silence.

Waiting for it, Davis ran across the opening and got to the oak table as a burst from the Uzis took fragments from the glass door and shattered a lamp. He got to the kitchen window with the Mauser 30–06, jacking a shell into the chamber. He got there in time and squeezed off two rounds at the figure running through the scrub toward the stock tank. The figure stopped dead, hesitated, and ran back, throwing himself behind a low rise. Davis stepped aside. A burst came through the kitchen window, blowing out the panes of glass.

He picked up dishtowels from the sink and moved back to the table to stuff 30–06 cartridges in his jacket, then picked up Tali's Beretta and skidded it across the floor, past the oriental rug to where she was kneeling over Rosen. With the rifle, the shotgun, and the old Enfield revolver, he ran back across the wide-open doorway, bringing a quick burst from the desert.

Rosen was propped against the wall, his chin on his chest, looking down at the blood soaking his jacket. The exit wound was just below the right breast.

"It went through you," Davis said.

Rosen looked up at him, glassy-eyed, his mouth open, as Davis opened his jacket and shirt and pressed a folded dishtowel against the wound. A bad one, a sucking chest wound, percolating air and blood. With splintered pieces of his ribs in the wound. Rosen's expression said he couldn't believe it. He was perspiring. A cold, clammy sweat. He was in shock.

"Turn over a little."

He helped Rosen roll his body so he could press a dishtowel against the entrance wound, which was small and showed very little blood, and then brought him back gently to lie on his back.

"We'll get you fixed up in a minute," Davis said. He took Rosen's right hand and laid it on the towel covering the air-sucking hole in his chest. "Here, keep your hand on it and press, just a little."

"I've been shot," Rosen said.

"You'll be okay. Try not to move."

"I *can't* move. Christ."

That was good, his tone. But he had to calm him down. "Don't fight to breathe. Try and relax."

"I brought them," Tali said. "I made this happen."

Davis glanced at her. "Take your gun, it's on the floor there. Go in the back bedroom and watch the other side of the house."

"They shoot him, it's my fault. . . ." She was looking at Rosen with an awful expression: pain, anguish, wanting to cry, wanting to lie down with Rosen and give up.

"Jesus Christ!" Davis said. "Will you get out in the goddamn bedroom? Go *on*." He picked up the Beretta and forced her to take it.

As she finally moved, he rose with the shotgun and fired both barrels past the edge of the doorway—for noise rather than in a hope of hitting them. There was no return fire, and when he looked he didn't see the figures in the scrub. He reloaded the shotgun and brought the Mauser with him, crawling a few steps to the nearest of the front windows. He had to rise up to push it open. Then he squatted again and laid the Mauser on the windowsill. There was no sign of their car. Nothing moved beyond the stone fence. No sounds from the other side of the house. He hoped she had qualified with a handgun. He hoped she wouldn't choke and freeze. Jesus Christ, he thought. What are you doing here? He let his gaze move back along the stone fence, then moved his position to the edge of the doorway and looked out. Nothing. He'd try them.

When he ducked past the opening to the other side, there was no gunfire. There was no movement. No sign of anything from the kitchen window. He moved through the hallway to the bedroom.

Tali stood between the side and back windows, holding the Beretta at her shoulder, the barrel pointing up. She looked over at him and seemed calm now.

"Anything?"

She shook her head. "Is he going to die?"

"I don't know."

"We have to get him to the hospital."

She said it so simply he stared at her and didn't know what to say.

"How're we gonna do that?"

"Tell them he's been shot. Tell them he's dying and they'll go away."

Was she that dumb? No, she was hoping. Or imagining a truce, a cease-fire to collect the wounded.

Maybe they did that in the desert. "They won't take our word," Davis said. "And if they come in to look, they'll finish him."

"Then what can we do?"

"See what the doctor's got. There's a medicine chest in the bathroom closet and some pills and stuff."

"He's going to be all right, isn't he?" Wanting him to say yes.

"I've seen a lot worse. You stay here, okay? But don't show yourself in the window."

She nodded and he turned away, going into the bathroom. He hoped there was morphine, though he didn't think the doctor would leave it in the house. The rib fragments would be like knife blades in him. Morphine would help. A goddamn sucking chest wound. He could tell by the sound, the wound trying to breathe, that Rosen had been shot through the lung.

THE JACKET WAS RUINED, the front of it dyed red in funny designs. The towel beneath his hand felt dry. With his fingers he had probed carefully beneath the towel and pulled his hand away when he felt something wet, something sharp and hard sticking out. Jesus. Something that was part of him. He didn't want to think about it, his body ripped open by a machine-gun bullet, blood pouring out. But it was good that he could think about it. He was here and able to think. He tasted blood in his mouth. He didn't know where the Marine was, or Tali. He had heard their voices before, the Marine yelling something. Not yelling, but his voice hard. It was easier to breathe when he relaxed. Before, he had thought he was suffocating, or drowning. Now it was easier and he felt less afraid of not being able to breathe, though he was nauseated and afraid he might throw up. The sound was still there when he breathed, like bubbles in a straw, but not that loud. It was difficult to move. It felt as if a spike had been driven through him, holding him to the floor. He felt the floor moving, someone walking. The Marine was close, kneeling now, looking at him.

"How you doing?"

"Christ, I got shot. You know it?"

The Marine had white towels and some other things in his arms, setting them on the floor.

"Let's get you fixed up," Davis said. "You're gonna have to roll over again, on your left side."

He felt the coat pulling and heard the scissors then.

"You cutting my jacket off?" Somewhat alarmed.

"You can get a new one," Davis said. He raised Rosen's arm to pull the right side of the jacket from Rosen's body. "Look at these. See if you know what they are." He put several bottles of pills, without labels, on the floor by Rosen's face. "You picked the right house. We've got compress bandages, sulfa powder—what do you see there?"

"Aspirin, tranquilizers . . . halizone tablets," Rosen said. "Dramamine, in case we get seasick. Where's Tali?" Again alarmed, remembering she was here.

"She's all right, she's in the bedroom. Hold still."

He got Rosen's wounds dressed, front and back, and brought him blankets and pillows—a pillow for his

head and one to elevate his feet—deciding this corner
of the front room might be the safest place in the
house.

Rosen felt the Marine walking across the floor
again. Then felt more vibrations with sounds that went
through him. He turned his head to look. The Marine
was moving furniture around. Christ, rearranging the
room. No, he was pushing the heavy couch and easy
chairs into the open doorway of the patio, turning
them over to form a flowery barricade of cushions.

"I'm thirsty," Rosen said.

He heard someone calling then, from outside.

"THE GODDAMN MARINE," Valenzuela said. "He's in there,
he's got no business being there. How much's he paying him? He could've left—you know what I mean?
He sees how it is, shit, he knows. But he comes back
here."

"He's paying him *something*," Rashad said. "Man
ain't doing it for the love of his country. Say he shoots
for money. We say to him how much does he want to
quit shooting, walk away and mind his business."

"I don't know," Valenzuela said. "If it's like that, if
he's got a price, then maybe we ought to find out."

Teddy came in a crouch along the stone fence to the
spot where they were sitting on the ground, near the
open gate. Teddy had stayed out there, looking for a
shot.

He said, "Well, what do you think?"

Valenzuela looked at him. "What do I think? What do *you* think, for Christ's sake?"

"I'm pretty sure we got him," Teddy said. "Didn't you see him? He stumbled, the Marine and the girl, it looked like both of them grabbed him."

"I didn't see him stumble," Valenzuela said. "I saw the Marine pull 'em into the house. Fucking Marine, I'll tell you."

"Listen, I know we hit him," Teddy said, "and I think it was me. I had it right on his back. You said go, I pinned him, I know it."

"If he was dead," Rashad said, "it would be over. They wouldn't have no reason to stay in the house."

"I didn't say he was dead," Teddy said. "No, but I'm pretty sure I hit him. You know, it looks like a setup. They're in the hole, nothing they can do. Trapped. But they got a place. They got food, water, whatever, and we're out here in the fucking rocks. What if somebody comes along? I mean we don't have time to sit around. If he's still alive, then we've got to finish it."

"Why don't you rush the house?" Rashad said. "All he's got is a rifle, a shotgun, and some other shit. He could even have the place mined. You know it?"

"We got to get him out of there," Valenzuela said.

"Or keep him busy," Teddy said. "Say if I could get up there close enough to plant a charge. One of you— how about this? One of you go up and talk to him. See if he'd just as soon go home alive. I'll take some stuff, see what I can do. Put a hole in the place and we drive in."

"Let's do it," Valenzuela said. He looked at Rashad. "Call him. Tell him you want to talk."

"You want me to do it?"

"You're his buddy," Valenzuela said. "Go on."

Rashad moved to the stone fence on his knees and gradually began to pull himself up.

"Hey, Marine!"

The rifle shot sang off the rim of stone and ricocheted into the desert. Rashad was on the ground again. He looked up at the top of the fence and at the sky.

"Hey, my man! . . . We not mad at you! We want to talk!"

RASHAD WAS WAVING something white, a handkerchief. Standing in the open gate now, testing him. Or testing himself.

Davis put the front sight of the Mauser on Rashad's chest.

Now the skinny one with the hair was coming out, starting up the drive with Rashad, both of them holding their hands out from their sides.

"No guns!" Rashad called.

Shoot them. It was in Davis' mind.

The third one appeared then, Valenzuela, standing up behind the stone fence that was waist-high on him. Valenzuela held his arms out.

Davis moved the rifle sight to the left a few inches, held in on Valenzuela, then moved it back to the two figures coming up the drive.

"Come on out and talk," Rashad said. He began to

angle across the coarse grass toward the house, still holding the white handkerchief. The one with the hair continued up the drive, looking toward the house, the three of them becoming more spread out as they approached. Maybe armed, but not with Uzis. Not Rashad or the one with the hair. Maybe pulling something, but not, apparently, coming to shoot.

Rashad said, "How's Mr. Rosen?" He waited. "If you ain't gonna talk, my man, how we gonna have a talk?"

Valenzuela was still moving along the fence. The one with the hair was approaching the rear of the black Mercedes, still looking toward the house.

Davis glanced over his shoulder. "Tali! Come here!" He looked at Rosen and saw his eyes open with a startled expression, the glassiness gone.

"What is it?" Rosen said. His eyes began to roll back again.

Rashad, in front of the house now, thirty meters away, said, "Hey, David, we got nothing against you, man. We got no reason to hurt you."

Tali, coming into the front room, said, "What? Is he all right?" Looking at Rosen, then seeing Davis at the window with the rifle.

"Watch the one in the driveway," Davis said. "Take the shotgun." The Kreighoff was next to him, leaning against the sill. "Can you shoot it?"

"I think so."

He watched her as she pushed a window open and raised the Kreighoff, extending it through the opening.

"Who's that," Rashad said, "Mr. Rosen? No, hey, that ain't Mr. Rosen, is it? Where's he at?"

"Get down," Davis said to Tali.

"Look," Rashad said then, "we got nothing against you or her either. The two of you can get in the car, man, and leave. But if you stay here . . . shit, you gonna die. You know that. For what? Some money? How much he paying you?"

Valenzuela had stopped. Now he was moving along the fence again, almost even with the patio. Fifty meters to Valenzuela.

Thirty to Rashad.

"David!" Tali's voice. "He's behind the car!"

Davis swung the Mauser. He could see the one with the hair through the side windows of the Mercedes. She should have fired and kept him back, but it was expecting too much. It would have happened too quickly for her.

Davis aimed at the rear-door window and fired and saw the window and the window on the other side fragment in a web of lines, drilled cleanly by the high-velocity 30–06, the figure back there suddenly gone. Rashad was running. Davis swung the Mauser on him, then went down as the windows exploded with the hard clatter of Valenzuela's weapon and pressed against the wall below the sill, seeing Tali on the floor with the shotgun, embracing it, holding on tight, her eyes squeezed closed. The sound stopped.

Davis rose up. He saw Rashad running for the gate. He saw Valenzuela behind the fence with the Uzi. He fired at Valenzuela, squeezing off two rounds, seeing him drop behind the fence, swung the Mauser and tried to nail Rashad with the two rounds he had left, but not in time. Rashad was through the gate. There was no sign of the third one. He had run off into the scrub, beyond the car.

"I TOOK a pretty good look," Valenzuela said. "I didn't see the hole we're supposed to drive a car through in the wall. In fact, I didn't hear any explosion at all."

"I changed my mind," Teddy said. "I think when I saw the rifle sticking out the window, fucking elephant gun. I started picturing what this guy must look like in his uniform with the ribbons and medals and I figured one of them said 'expert.' Not somebody throwing wild shots, *expert*. Fucking Marines, they got all that shit on them, all the medals. But wait." Teddy had a cigarette in his hand and paused before lighting it, looking from Valenzuela to Rashad. "Did I come back empty-handed? You bet I did."

"What'd you do with it?" Valenzuela said.

"I stuck a wad under the left rear fender. The wire goes out into the bushes over there."

"What's that do for us?" Valenzuela said.

"Blow the car. Show 'em they're not going anywhere."

"Or wait and see if they try and *use* the car," Rashad said. "Thinking they can sneak out across the desert after it gets dark. Man, if we gonna be here that long—and I don't see why we won't."

It was a good possibility. Teddy left in the gray

Mercedes—parked down the wadi from the stone
fence—to run into Eilat and get some supplies, some
food and something to drink, like ice-cold beer.
They'd never felt the sun press so hot. Got them cor-
nered, Rashad said, and we the ones dying of thirst.

He said to Valenzuela, after Teddy had left, "They
can stay in there a week, but we can't stay out here. We
can cut the electric wire, it wouldn't hurt them none.
We can mess up their water pump, they probably got
something else to drink. You understand what I'm
saying?"

"We got to get to the Marine," Valenzuela said.
"Christ, I know that."

"Yeah, but with something he can see," Rashad
said. "We tell him we don't want to kill him. What
does he think about that? It's not something he can see
and say yeah, I want that. It's only driving away from
here, having in his head he left Rosen. You understand? But we offer him something good—hey, look at
this—then he's got something else in his head when he
drives off. Or when he thinks he's gonna drive off."

"Offer him money," Valenzuela said. "What else?"

"No, that's it, money. But how much we got? You
gonna write him a check? But see, we offer him a
whole *pile* of money, then his head starts working and
he can give himself excuses for leaving, like, we gonna
get Rosen anyway . . . he can't stay with Rosen the rest
of his life . . . he's not responsible for the man. Things
like that. He can take something from us and say why
not, the man's gonna die anyway."

"Where's the pile of money?" Valenzuela said.

"I believe the lawyer's got it," Rashad said. "How big a pile, I don't know, but the Arab kid said he had money, my buddy. See, after the money was supposed to've been delivered the lawyer's still here. Least he was yesterday. So I don't believe he delivered it. I believe the lawyer's still got Rosen's money, waiting for Rosen to come get it."

"We don't know that," Valenzuela said.

"No, but there's a way we can find out," Rashad said. "How long's it take to drive to Tel Aviv, four hours?"

Valenzuela pulled the highway map out of his coat pocket and, sitting with his back to the stone fence, opened it to the mileage chart.

"Three hundred and forty-two kilometers." Valenzuela began to nod, estimating time and distance. "Yeah, you could be back here in eight, nine hours. It's an idea. Maybe bring Mel with you."

"I was thinking that," Rashad said. "Use him to talk, so we won't be exposing our bodies. Standing out there, man, playing the friendly nigger, that ain't my style."

HOLDING THE MAUSER on the stone fence fifty yards away, knowing they were there, behind the fence or maybe in the shade of some scrub, he imagined telling Master Sergeant T. C. Cox about it.

"See, they came up the drive with their hands held out from their sides, showing they were unarmed. The other one was over behind the wall."

T. C. Cox: The ones trying to kill you.

Davis: Yeah, trying to kill this Rosen.

T. C. Cox: Trying to kill you too, as I understand it.

Davis: Well, at this point it looked like they wanted to talk.

T. C. Cox: What was there to talk about? They wanted to kill you.

Davis: See, the girl was covering the one with the hair, but he got behind the car.

T. C. Cox: He got behind the car. What'd you let him do that for?

Davis: Well, the girl was watching him.

T. C. Cox: I thought you watched the both of them come up the drive.

Davis: I did.

T. C. Cox: Then why didn't you kill them?

Davis didn't hear himself say anything.

T. C. Cox: What were you waiting for?

Davis: All that sitting around the embassy like a bank guard . . .

T. C. Cox: You had the chance. Why didn't you kill them?

It scared hell out of him. How fast you could forget how to react.

22

DURING THE AFTERNOON he changed Rosen's dressing. There was very little blood now, but the wound bubbled and sucked air when he uncovered it and put on another compress. He knew Rosen heard the sound.

"I'm breathing out of both ends," Rosen said. He rinsed his mouth with water and spit it in the pan Davis had placed next to him. There was a milk bottle for when he had to take a leak, but he hadn't used it yet.

"I'm not supposed to drink, how about if I smoke?"

"Your lung's got enough trouble," Davis said.

"I won't inhale. No, it'd be a good time to quit. You know how many times I've quit in the last year? That goddamn fire—you know, I started smoking again right after that. Pack and a half a day...hey... what's gonna happen?"

"I'm going out when it gets dark," Davis said.

"Get help? The police?"

"It'd take too long, a couple hours or more. I just

want to look around. I've got some plastic in my car, but not much wire and no way to fire it, unless we hook it to a light switch. But that would be if we were pretty desperate. Get them coming in. Your car's sitting out there. Tali says she left the key in it. Maybe that's a way, if we can get you to the car. Shoot out through the back. But I don't know—shit, there isn't any road back there. It's all rocks and gullies. The other thing, one of them was by your car and he might've rigged it with a charge. I don't know, but I better find out."

"Or tell them okay, you'll leave," Rosen said. "Take Tali and get out of here. I appreciate it—listen, you don't know, but this doesn't have anything to do with you."

"You want them to shoot Tali?"

"That's what I'm talking about, if she stays here. If *you* stay," Rosen said.

"You think we walk out there they won't shoot us? Alive, we're witnesses. Dead, we go in the same hole you do."

"We're gonna get out," Rosen said. "Right?"

Davis nodded.

"I mean what I said—I'm gonna give you something," Rosen said. "In fact you can name it. Anything I've got, you can have." Rosen was silent a moment. "Listen, if I die . . ."

"If you want to live, then live," Davis said. "That's what you do. You don't think about anything else."

"It's funny the things you do think about." Rosen smiled. "Dr. Morris comes home—holy shit, what happened to my house? I keep seeing his face. Thinking about the expenses I'm gonna have, then it isn't so funny."

"You need a couple of windows in your car," Davis said.

"And the other one, the gray one—Christ, how about those guys using my car?—I imagine it's all shot up." Rosen shook his head. "It's funny what you think about. It's funny I'm not more scared. But I think, well, whatever happens—it's interesting because something like this, you can imagine, has never happened to me before. Like watching it and not being in it. Is that how you look at it? I was thinking how it might be in combat. It's always the other guy who's gonna get hit, isn't it? Well, okay, whatever happens. It's interesting . . . I know a guy had a lung collapse on him. He said it hurt like a sonofabitch, something about the lining—I didn't understand that part—but he said they pumped it back up. I guess I got some broken ribs, too. Well, I had that before in a car accident. Rear-end collision, I went into the fucking steering wheel. But they're all broken off, aren't they?"

"The wound's clean," Davis said. "We keep it clean, everything else can be fixed."

"I'm glad you know what you're doing," Rosen said. "You may not feel the same way, but I'm glad you're here. As I told you once before—Christ, just last night, it seems like a week ago—you'll make it. You've got a nice natural style."

———

"HOW DO YOU SPELL IT?" Mel said to the girl sitting next to him at the Pal Hotel bar. She was fairly good-looking—dark skin, rosy makeup, and black black hair. Mel figured she would have a very heavy black bush. He liked that.

When she had spelled her name for him he said, "That's Guela. Ga-way-la."

"No, no," the girl said. "Geh-oo-lah. Say it."

"Gay-woo-la," Mel said. "That's Jewish, huh?"

"Yes, Hebrew."

"I never heard it before. Isaac?"

Itzak, the barman, came over. "Yes, please, Mr. Bondy."

"Same way. Campari and soda. Give her one."

The girl smiled and thanked him and moved a little closer, hanging her hip off the stool to touch his thigh.

"Save it," Mel said. "I'm buying a drink. We haven't agreed I'm buying anything else. How much?"

"Four hundred lira." Quietly, close to him.

"Your ass."

"Yes?"

"That means you're high. It's too much."

"Too much? The same as fifty dollar."

"The same as fifty dollar is three hundred lira," Mel said. "Today's rate of exchange at the Bank of Israel, determined by the devaluation of the common-market dollar discount. And if you believe that, we can go upstairs and fall in love."

"All right," the girl said. "Three hundred lira."

"How many times?"

"How many times? One time. How many times you good to do it for?"

That's how it happened that Rashad found Mel with his white ass up in the air, his face buried in a pillow, and Guelah doing her routine, moaning and gasping with her eyes open.

Rashad pressed the barrel of the Beretta into Mel's left buttock and said, "Now, if you can keep going, my man, *that's* savoir faire."

ROSEN SAID to Tali, who was sitting close to him in the darkness, "I'm gonna tell you something I never told anybody before."

"Yes?"

"I'm part Jewish." He waited.

Tali said again, "Yes?"

"Well, are you surprised?"

"I always think you are a Jew," Tali said. "What does it mean *part?* Part of what?"

"You thought I was? Why?"

"I don't know." Tali shrugged. "I always think it. Your appearance . . ."

"Come on."

"Your name . . ."

"My name, I made up the name. You know who I really am? Baptized? James C. Ross. Jimmy Ross. But most people, even my wife, called me Ross."

"It's a nice name, Ross. It's not Hebrew?"

"I don't know, I guess some people named Ross are Jewish, but I didn't know that, because my mother was

Irish, her name was Connelly, and she was always talking about the Irish, like there was something special about them, a gift, or talking about her people coming from Cork. So I thought Ross was Irish almost all my life. Then when my dad died—I was nineteen, I came home from the service for the funeral—I found out our name originally was Rosen. My dad's grandfather changed it when he came over from England. But see, nobody on my dad's side ever practiced the Jewish faith, so I didn't know anything about it till I came here. And you know what? It's interesting. I don't buy all the kosher business, Christ, the diet laws. What does Almighty God care if you eat butter with steak? He's got enough to think about, all the fuck-ups in the world. But the history and all, it's interesting."

"My name, Atalia, is from the history time."

"Is that right? I thought it meant from Italy."

"No, it's from very far back, but I don't read about it in a long time."

"See, you're the new breed," Rosen said. "You can't be bothered with religion, all the ceremony."

"We have our meal together, the family, on Friday evening," Tali said. "I still want you to meet my mother sometime."

"What do I want to meet your mother for? She fool around?"

"No, of course not."

"What do you mean, of course not. You probably don't even know her. You ever talk to her about what she feels and thinks, what you feel? Kids don't know their parents. They grow up and start thinking about them as real people after they're dead. People waste time, years, playing games with each other—who am I?—and never get to know anybody."

"Is this true?" Tali said.

"Yes, it's true," Rosen said. "I think I'm getting close to something, a truth about how to live life and not waste it or mess up. I'll get it clear in my mind and tell you about it."

"I would like to hear that," Tali said. "Learn what to do with my life before I get old."

"It's simple," Rosen said. "It's not easy, but it's simple."

WHEN TALI ROSE and moved away he could hear the Marine talking to her. Then the Marine came over—feeling his steps on the floor—and crouched down next to him. He could see the Marine's face in the light from the window as the Marine stared outside. Looking down at him, the Marine's features vanished in the dark.

"You want to know something?"

"What?" the Marine said.

"I never told anybody this before and you may not believe it, but I'm part Jewish."

"Yeah?"

The Marine didn't seem impressed.

"I don't mean I'm a convert. I mean I was born part Jewish, on my father's side."

"Is that right?"

"You don't believe me."

"I never thought you weren't Jewish," the Marine said. "Listen, I'm going out again. I looked around back, there's nobody there, like they don't think we'd try to leave that way. I don't know if it does us any good, I've got to see if we might use your car first. Or see if I can catch them asleep or looking the other way. I don't think they're much for watch-standing. You hang in there and we'll get this thing done soon as we can."

"Why'd you think I was Jewish?" Rosen said.

IT WAS NOT the same darkness as Indochina. The sky seemed wider and closer here because of the desert. The shadows seemed different, or there were fewer shadows because there was less vegetation. He would have to get used to the shadows. Then he hoped he wouldn't be here long enough to learn a new set of shadows.

Going out of the doctor's house was not the same as going out of a helicopter after sitting with his eyes closed during the fifteen- or twenty-minute flight, opening his eyes and going out blackfaced with a recon patrol. It was different. But he was not afraid of being alone in dark places. The difference here was that he knew what the enemy looked like. They had faces. And they knew what he looked like and could be expecting him, even dressed in Dr. Morris' black coat sweater and dark gray trousers. He had taken his cap off for the first time in two days.

It was three-twenty A.M. when he left the house.

He moved around back, past the dry stock tank that might have been used at one time for goats or sheep. Or maybe the doctor had kept horses. The blades at the top of the windmill structure stood motionless. The desert was empty, its shadows motionless. People were close, but there were no sounds and nothing moved. He had said to Tali, "Don't shoot me when I go by a window or when I come back."

From the side of the house he moved into the carport, working his way along between the tarp-covered Camaro and the cement wall. He thought about going under the tarp to get the C4 on the back seat. But what would he do with it if he couldn't run out a line and explode it? Shooting the plastic with a bullet wouldn't set it off. It took an electrical charge. Or what would he do if he got under the tarp and they knew he was there? They'd wrap him up in it. So leave the C4.

The black Mercedes was down the drive about twenty meters, almost halfway to the gate in the stone fence. (He remembered Tali stopping there when they arrived, wondering why she hadn't driven up to the house. But then he remembered she had seen Rosen coming from the patio and had stopped abruptly and jumped out to run to meet him.) From the carport he studied the black Mercedes gleaming in the darkness, about forty thousand dollars' worth of car in Israel. Rosen had a pretty good life. It wouldn't be hard to get to the car. Davis slipped his hand into the unbuttoned top of the coat sweater and drew his Colt.

On his belly now, using elbows and knees, he moved from the carport to the front bumper of the

Mercedes. He listened. He rolled to his back and inched under the car, using his heels now, moving close to the wheels on one side because the spine of the driveway was high between the wheel ruts. His hand moved over the underbody and frame. He didn't think he would find anything. The one with the hair hadn't had time to get underneath. The guy hadn't opened a door, Davis was pretty sure of that. He pulled himself out on the desert side of the Mercedes, remained low, and felt along the rocker panel to the rear-wheel housing, feeling inside the fender above the left rear wheel and there it was, a hunk of plastic with the wire coming down and trailing out to the side. The guy hadn't tried to hide the wire; he hadn't had time. The wire was wedged beneath the tire and led off across the gravel to the edge of the property, where the detonator would be. Or else the wire made a turn there, around the base of a tree, and continued down toward the front of the property, to the stone fence. That was more likely, so the guy would be there with his buddies and not have to sit off in the scrub. They'd be nervous and want to be together. They were from a city. They'd sit out here in the bush and see things and have to be cool in front of one another.

They were somewhere behind the stone fence. Davis had to assume that. The fence was protection. They weren't spread out the way they should be—the way he would have positioned them—so they were back there. He hoped they were close behind the fence, near the gate. If they were, there was a good chance of finishing it.

He holstered the Colt, then pried the C4 from be-neath the curve of the wheel housing and pulled out the blasting cap attached to the wire. Belly-down again, with the end of the wire in one hand and the hunk of plastic in the other, he began inching along the driveway toward the stone fence. He hoped there was enough wire. He wouldn't have to go all the way. . . .

Get close enough. Stick the cap in the plastic again and throw it against the stone fence.

They might hear it, they might not.

He'd be moving then, back to the Mercedes. Reach in and turn the key.

They'd hear the engine start.

The one with the hair would run to his detonator.

The other two would come to the stone fence.

Davis got to within ten meters of the fence. He waited, listening, pulled the wire toward him, slowly, bringing it across the gravel and coarse grass, then planted the blasting cap in the ball of plastic. Rising to his knees, he again drew the Colt out of the sweater. He threw the ball of plastic underhand and watched it arc toward the fence. It disappeared in darkness against the stones.

He was moving back toward the Mercedes when he heard the sound, a faraway groaning sound—a car la-boring in low gear—coming from somewhere in the desert. He looked back. Beyond the fence and past a stand of trees, a beam of light was reflecting off the rocks.

23

ALL THAT TIME being Jimmy Ross had been a long time. It seemed longer than the twenty-five years or more he was just Ross. He had been Rosen hardly any time at all.

Growing up, it was a matter of always looking into the future for something, always hoping or planning for something, never knowing when you would get there and not knowing it when you did. Jimmy Ross to Ross to Rosen. He wondered what the real Al Rosen was doing, if he was still in Cleveland.

All right, this Rosen was here. He had finally made it. It had taken him fifty years to learn that *being* was the important thing. Not being something. Just being. Looking around you and knowing you were being, not preparing for anything. That was a long time to learn something. He should have known about it when he was seven, but nobody had told him. The only thing they'd told him was that he had to be *some*thing. See, if he'd known it then, he'd have had all that time to enjoy being. *Except it doesn't have anything to do with time*, he thought. Being is an hour or a minute or even a moment. Being is being, no matter where you are. In a house in the Sinai desert at night. But if you have to be somewhere, why not be somewhere good?

Sitting by the pool at the Laromme. In another few weeks it would be too hot, unbearable, in Eilat.

Netanya, on the Mediterranean.

Or go over to one of the Greek islands. See if there was a difference between Hydra tourist ladies and Mykonos tourist ladies.

No, he had done that, the tourist-lady comparing. Do something else.

Or don't do anything. Sit. You don't have to do anything, he told himself. You don't have to prove anything.

"Avoid running at all times. And never look back. Something might be gaining on you." Rules for success and happiness courtesy of Satchel Paige, who had missed playing with the Original Al Rosen by a couple of years.

Make sense?

Yes, of course. Tali said that. Yes, of course. Tali was nice and it would be nice to tell her things and watch her nod seriously and then laugh when she saw he was kidding. But that was planning and he wasn't going to plan. He was going to do nothing. He began to think that it would be better to do nothing in the sunlight than in the dark. Thinking was doing something. He wished he could stop thinking. He wished it wasn't dark. He wished he wasn't nailed to the floor and could move. He wished he could swallow some water. He wished he wasn't cold. He wished he didn't feel as if he were drowning. He wished he hadn't talked to the government lawyers. No, he thought then, you had to have done all that to be where you are and know what you know. Unless he could have learned the same thing serving a one-to-five at Lewisburg for conspiring to defraud the United States Government. With time off for good behavior. Yes, he was pretty sure he could have learned it at Lewisburg. The point being that learning required a change of attitude and sometimes, usually, pain. He knew that but wasn't sure how he knew it. He wondered if it would do any good if he called out for his mother. Shit, Rosen thought. Just when he was getting there.

24

(TWO THINGS WERE HAPPENING at the same time.)
The wheels of the gray Mercedes, Mati driving, had
skidded off the wadi trail into deep sand. The left rear
wheel was spinning as Mati gunned it and as Rashad
and Valenzuela grunted, trying to push the car out with
their hands. Valenzuela was asking Rashad why he had
let the Arab kid drive, for Christ's sake, and Rashad
said because he was a driver, it's what he did, and had
driven fine all the way from Tel Aviv. Then Valenzuela
blew up, realizing Mel was sitting on his fat ass in the
front seat with Mati while he and Rashad were doing
the work. He yelled at Mel to get his ass out here, then
said to Mati okay, hold it, turn it off for a minute. They
were down the wadi trail a short distance. Around the
next bend and past the stand of trees was the stone
fence. Valenzuela looked up to see Teddy, his submachine gun slung over his shoulder, standing in the low
headlight beams.

(The other thing that was happening, in the yard of

the desert house, was that Davis was reaching into the black Mercedes to turn on the ignition.)

Valenzuela said, "Hey, would you like to come help us?"

"I thought I heard something," Teddy said.

They all heard it then: the sound of a car engine starting.

Teddy turned and was gone.

Valenzuela had to stop and look around for his Uzi lying on the ground and pick it up. And Rashad hesitated a moment, looking at Mel standing there and thinking about Mel's attaché case in the back seat of the car. So the two of them started off well behind Teddy.

They got to the bend in the road and saw Teddy reach the gate and cut left, over into the scrub where he had hidden his detonator box. They saw the black car up in the yard and could hear the engine rumbling and in that moment Rashad saw something else, a figure, something, moving across the yard toward the patio. He paused to pull his Beretta and began firing as Valenzuela saw the movement and opened up with the Uzi, spraying bursts at the front of the house. The pause saved their lives.

Teddy, looking at the black Mercedes, turned the switch on his detonator box.

A twelve-foot section of the stone fence exploded in a black shower of sand and smoke and rock fragments.

Valenzuela was hit by bits of rock and took Rashad with him over the edge of the cutbank into the wadi.

They tried to cover their heads as the hard fragments pelted down on them.

Rashad was up first. He found Teddy in the bushes with blood coming out of his dusty hair, streaming down his face, still holding the detonator box. Now Valenzuela was partway out of the wadi, firing over the bank at the front of the house, raking the windows until the clip was empty.

Rashad said to Teddy, "Say you the explosives expert, huh? Say shit."

DAVIS WAITED on the patio until the machine-gun fire stopped. He rose by the tipped-over couch and reached into the darkness of the room.

"Tali, hand me the rifle." She sat looking down at Rosen and began to turn only when he said, "Come on, give me it!" and reached for the Mauser leaning against the front windowsill.

Handing it to him, she said, "David—"

"Stick the shotgun out and keep watching. I'm gonna try and scare something up, see if we got any of them."

"David—" Her voice low, subdued.

But he was gone, across the patio and moving in a low crouch into the desert, still hearing her voice, the sound of it—no excited questions about the explosion—and then she was gone from his mind as he reached patches of scrub growth and made his way down to the stone fence, to the place where it ended and wire strung between posts continued out into the desert.

He went over the wall crouched, looking down the length of wedged, fitted stones to the rubble of broken stones he could see as an outline, a mound in the darkness. There were shapes he did not wait to study, something moving. Davis opened fire, squeezing off five solid rounds, hearing them sing off the rocks, and went over the wall into the yard and crouched low again as he reloaded the Mauser. He waited, but there were no sounds, only what was left of a ringing sensation close to his head. He waited a quarter of an hour for some sign from them, but heard nothing.

Davis returned to the house the way he had come, crossed the cement patio, and stepped over the sofa barricading the doorway.

Tali rose from the corner, coming to him out of deep shadow.

"I try to tell you about Mr. Rosen," Tali said.

Davis looked down, seeing only Rosen's legs in the faint light from the window.

"How is he?"

"He died," Tali said.

25

MAYBE THEY'D USED to wail and pull their hair. The Marine thought of that. The girl was making herself feel responsible, punishing herself, not crying much but making sounds as though she were in pain. It wasn't a reasonable laying of blame, it was more like a rite: working herself up to feel guilt and anguish.

The Marine held her and stroked her gently, feeling a little self-conscious, staring out the window and across the yard to the stone line, the boundary.

Finally he sat her on the floor by the window and looked at Rosen, his hands one over the other holding the clean compress bandage. He felt Rosen's throat for a pulse, then closed his eyelids, listening to the girl string *if*s together: if she had realized . . . if she had gone to the police instead of the hotel . . . if she had been alert and not led them here . . . The Marine was patient for a while; he gave her time. He sat with her and put his arm around her, bringing her close to him, as he would comfort a child, occasionally making his own sounds—"I'm sorry . . . I know how you feel, but . . . no, don't say that . . ."—trying to ease her sounds of pain. She would say things to him in Hebrew in the mournful tone and it would sound even more ceremonial to him, from a time thousands of years ago when a man had died in the desert and the women huddled by a fire. He tried to think of things to say to her that would help. Her eyes were closed, squeezed closed. He wondered how long she would keep it up, if she would stop abruptly or just wind down from exhaustion and fall asleep. He didn't know what to say that would help or what to do other than hold her. She told him she wanted to die. She told him Mr. Rosen would be alive if it weren't for her. She told him Mr. Rosen had trusted her and she had failed him and now she couldn't live with herself anymore.

He said to her, "He's dead. What you do to yourself doesn't change it."

She wasn't listening to him. She said, "He was going to be safe. Go to Sharm el Sheikh or Santa Katarina and stay there and be safe with me to help him. He said to me, he called me to come and said, 'Atalia, I want you to have something.' He said in his billfold was the key to the safe box of his bank. He said he wanted me to have it, to sign his name the way he signed it, with the initials, and take out the money. I said, 'Why? It's your money.' He said, 'No, now it's yours.' I said, 'But why?' He didn't say anything more. I went away to look out the windows—"

"Then he knew it," Davis said.

"I came back . . . I felt him, I breathe in his mouth. . . ."

He took her face in his hand and raised it to look at him and waited until her eyes opened.

"He's dead," Davis said. "They killed him." Her eyes closed and she tried to turn her head. "Look at me. *They* killed him."

"But it wouldn't have happen . . ."

"Look at me!"

Her eyes opened—her face close enough to see into her eyes and what she was feeling, the little girl experiencing something beyond her imagination, in a place she had never been before.

"They killed him," Davis said. "But they don't know it."

She was listening now, beginning to come back into the world. "We tell them?"

Davis shook his head. "No, we don't tell them."

"But if we say we want to take his body with us for burial, they would understand. Everyone respects that."

Davis' hand relaxed and brushed her cheek as he let it drop to her shoulder.

"I think if they knew he was dead they'd leave and wouldn't bother about us. Mr. Rosen said it was like a business with them. They don't have personal feelings about it. If it's done, then they're not gonna sit out there in the heat just to get at us. See, I don't think they care. I don't think they're afraid of what would happen if we told on them. They'd already be gone."

"I don't understand," the girl said. "We don't do anything?"

"I don't want them to leave yet," Davis said.

"Why?"

"I'd like to talk to them again."

"But why?"

He was staring out the window at the first trace of morning, pale strips of light rising beyond the desert and the sea and the Arabian mountains.

"I've got something to say to them," Davis said.

"Call to them to come out."

"I don't know yet how I want to say it," Davis said. "But I will."

Tali made coffee and sat with her cup, staring at Mr. Rosen, remembering him saying funny things to her. At times she would smile. She didn't bother the Marine now, who sat with his legs folded and his back sloping, staring out the window at the yard and at the opening in the stone fence that was wider now with part of it blown away. She let him be with himself.

VALENZUELA'S SHOULDER HURT where he had fallen on it going into the wadi. His head hurt, too, but not as much as Teddy's. Teddy needed stitches. He had tied a patterned scarf around his head and with his hair and bodyshirt he looked like an art deco pirate.

Rashad was the only one who sat on the cutbank of the wash and seemed to enjoy the lukewarm beer and dry-roasted peanuts they had for breakfast. He was very patient. He had let Valenzuela sleep and wake up stiffly to see the morning before showing Val and Teddy all the money in the alligator briefcase. Courtesy of Mel, the little lawyer, sitting over there inside the gray Mercedes that would be like an expensive oven pretty soon. Mel inside and his keeper, the Arab kid, sitting in the sand outside the car, playing with the sand, picking up a handful and letting it sift through a fist like time running out. Rashad liked the picture.

He said, "What's a little temporary discomfort when it's almost done? This is the number gonna bring him out, a hundred and ninety-five." And he tapped the alligator skin of the briefcase, doing a drum roll with his fingers. "Then, I assume, we gonna cut it? Otherwise, I'll tell you I thought about it seriously, I'd never have brought it."

"We cut it," Valenzuela said. "Comes to what? Sixty-something."

"Sixty-five each," Rashad said, "a day's wage." He looked over at Teddy. "Make your head feel better?"

"You want to know something?" Teddy said. "That fence blew, I got fucking stoned. With real stones, man." Yeah, he was feeling better, grinning, thinking sixty-five and five for the job was seventy and he wouldn't have to blow anybody up for two years. He said to Valenzuela, "We don't have to renegotiate, Val, I think this'll be fine."

"You like the picture?" Rashad said. "We use the man's car, now we using the man's bread to take the man out. It's like he's committing suicide, huh? Killing himself with his own bread. Lawyer says to me, 'What money? I don't have no money.' Standing there bare-ass pleading no, I don't have no money, and the whore, she's like this on the bed, leaning on her elbow?"— Rashad placed his open palm against the side of his face—"and with the other hand she's scratching her cooz, listening to us, don't even know she's doing it."

"That lawyer," Teddy said, "I think he likes to go around naked. Time we went to see him he was bare-ass."

"Cuz of his beautiful body," Rashad said. "He like to show it to people. He saying, 'What money, man?' It's under the bed with his airplane ticket. He say, 'Oh, the *comp*'ny money.' He was taking that back to the *comp*'ny today."

Valenzuela wasn't joining in or smiling. He was thinking about the money, yes—sixty-five each, that was all right, he'd split with them and it wouldn't matter to Harry, he'd get a kick out of it, using Rosen's money—but he was also thinking about the Marine.

"How much do we offer him?"

Rashad looked over. "All of it. The whole thing."

"He's gonna smell something," Valenzuela said.

"Sure he is, he's gonna smell money," Rashad said. "We let him look at it and feel it. There it is, sitting on the ground. Pick it up, man. Walk over to your car and drive away."

"Why would we offer him that much?" Valenzuela said. "Don't we want any? I'm talking about what he's thinking."

"Tell him the truth, it's Rosen's money," Rashad said. "We not out anything. See, he knows how much there is. What Mel say, he delivered five of the two hundred grand was sent here. So, we tell him the truth. Here's the rest of it. It ain't our money, he can have it if he walks away. Enough to retire on for life."

"What if he can't be bought?" Valenzuela said.

Rashad shook his head. "Who can't be bought? Name somebody. Shit, we got enough here to buy the whole United States Marines."

"He's gonna see it," Valenzuela said. "It isn't, you know, realistic, handing him that much money."

"That's the whole idea," Rashad said. "Make his eyes big and fuck up his head. When we talking about that much—look, it's sitting right there—the man knows he's taking a chance. See, it's got to be enough to take a chance *for*."

"No." Valenzuela was shaking his head now. "It's too much. There's a limit. You go over it and it isn't real or even possible anymore. Something in his head right away'd say no, don't touch it."

"All right, then don't offer him the whole thing," Rashad said. "Offer him what?"

"Half," Valenzuela said. "A hundred grand. It's a big number, but it sounds real, you know? Also it sounds like we're letting him in on something. We've talked it over and decided to split with him, like we're partners. We're all in it together. You see what I mean?"

"Yeah." Rashad was nodding. "I think maybe you're right. Like we're bringing him in. Uh-huh, so he can feel he's in it enough and can trust us, but not far enough he's helping to kill the man. Yeah, let his head work out that part of it."

"Gene—"

It was Mel's voice, Mel inside the gray Mercedes looking out at them.

"Hey, can I talk to you?"

"Probably has to go pee-pee," Rashad said. "Two times we had to stop so he could go in the ditch."

"You want to use him, huh?" Valenzuela said.

"You want to walk up to the house?" Rashad said. "The Marine gets nervous—that's fine, me and Teddy'll split the money. The lawyer can do it fine. Tell the Marine whatever we want to say."

Valenzuela waved to Mel to come over. They watched him get out of the car squinting, mopping his face with a handkerchief, adjusting the crotch of his light blue trousers, very busy as he approached them.

Rashad said, "Hot enough for you?"

"Man, this is a vacation spot, huh? Eilat?"

"Down closer to the water," Rashad said.

"I know dis ain't de place." Mel was being one of the boys. He said, "You know, I'm supposed to be on a TWA flight out of here—out of Tel Aviv, I mean—at nine o'clock. But doesn't look like I'm gonna make it, does it? I gave up trying to see Rosie. I decided stay out of it; it isn't any of my business."

"You might see him anyway," Valenzuela said, "but the man we want you to talk to is the Marine."

Mel opened his hands to show his innocence. "Look, I got nothing to do with this. What do you want to get me involved for?"

"He doesn't ever know nothing. One of those guys who doesn't know anything," Valenzuela said.

"Have I interfered with you in any way?" Mel said. "Have I given you any trouble? No, I've stayed out of it. You've got the money, okay, I can be very realistic about that. It's company funds. I gave the money to Rosie and something happened to it. It's too bad, I tell the company, but it's their problem or Rosie's. I mean I'm not out anything personally."

"He doesn't want to get involved," Valenzuela said.

"I'm *not* involved. You know that as well as I do."

"He gonna tell the comp'ny we took it from him and the comp'ny tell the FBI or somebody," Rashad said, playing with Mel.

"For what? What good's that do anybody?" Mel said, standing in the hot sun in the Sinai desert with two guys who killed people and didn't believe him. "Look, the company gave it to me to give to Rosen. Okay, as far as anybody knows, I gave it to him. That's the only thing I tell. Otherwise, shit, they might think I kept the money and put it somewhere for a rainy day."

"Which was your original idea," Rashad said.

"Okay, you're gonna think what you want," Mel said. "But believe this, because it's true. There's no way in the world I could finger you or testify against you. I mean even if I wanted to. Because there's no way in the world a complaint could be filed against you in court. What court? Here? Who's the complaint? Not me. In the U.S.? No way. Where are the witnesses? The proof? It would be strictly hearsay, my word against yours. But you think I'd ever be irritated enough to make a statement? What do I get out of that? As I said, I'm not out anything personally and I've kept my nose out of it because it's none of my business. So what more can I say?"

Mel raised his hands in a helpless gesture, looking from Rashad to Valenzuela to Teddy Cass and back to Valenzuela.

"Gene . . . how can I help you?"

"You can quit talking," Valenzuela said. "Clarence'll tell you what you're gonna do."

THERE HAD BEEN a car down by the wadi. Davis was sure he had heard a car, and headlight beams reflected on the rocks. Probably the gray car. One of them had gone to get something, a case of Maccabee and three pizzas to go. One of them could've been sleeping by the wall. Or back somewhere. One of them had triggered the detonator and that one could have also been by the wall. So he might have gotten one, maybe two of them. But he couldn't count on it. There was no way to find out except go down there.

It was eight o'clock, a bright, still morning, the sky filled with glare, cloudless.

Tali, sitting by Rosen's body, looked up as the Marine rose from the window and walked away. He came back unfolding a blanket and draped it over Rosen's body, beginning at his feet, bringing it up, then stopping as he reached Rosen's hands folded on his chest. He knelt down across from her. She watched him turn

Rosen's body, reach beneath him, and draw a billfold from the back pocket.

What he was doing gave her a terrible feeling. She couldn't believe it, the Marine looking in Mr. Rosen's wallet and bringing out money. When he tried to hand her the money she drew back and said "No!" surprised at the loudness of her voice.

"Take it. Five thousand dollars and a little more," Davis said. "Here's the key to his bank deposit box."

"I can't."

"You want to bury it with him? Would that make sense?"

"I can't take his money."

"He's giving it to you," Davis said. "You have to take it."

"But in the safe box he had very much money," Tali said. "And this, it's too much for me."

"He told me himself," Davis said, "you have to learn to accept money without your pride getting in the way. He's giving it to you because he liked you, he loved you, so don't insult him and try and change things when he's not here. Do whatever you want with the money. Buy clothes, take tap-dancing lessons if you want. But take it and thank God you knew the man."

He handed her the money and the key, then pulled the blanket up over Rosen, covering his face.

"I didn't know him very long, but I think he taught me a few things." Davis paused, thought for a moment, and said, "The wake's over."

Tali was looking at the money, holding it in front of her. "Will you take some of it?"

She didn't get an answer.

The voice came to them from outside; it was the black one, Rashad, calling out, "Hey, Marine! Here's somebody want to see you!"

26

"NO SHOOTING, man! Time's out!"

Rashad stood up at the wall, testing the Marine, giving him a moment.

"You hear? Man's lawyer wants to come out! Have a talk with you!"

He dropped behind the smooth stones again and waited. There was no answer from the house. He didn't expect one. All he wanted to do was get the Marine's attention. He didn't particularly care if the Marine shot Mel thinking it was somebody else, except then they'd have to talk to the Marine some other way, directly, and standing out there wasn't any fun. Now he crawled back to the thicket of dusty trees before rising and moving around the bend in the road to where they were waiting: Valenzuela and Teddy with their machine guns slung over their shoulders, the scared-looking lawyer with his resort outfit on standing between them, holding the alligator case. Mati, the

Arab-looking kid, was hunkered down over by the cut-bank, watching.

Rashad waved for Mel to come on. "Okay, go on up there and give your speech. But stay in the yard. You understand? He invites you in the house, you say, 'No thank you.'"

"I tell him and I come right back," Mel said. "That's all."

"You show him the money," Valenzuela said, "and wait and hear what he says."

Mel nodded quickly. "Okay. And then I come right back."

"Open the briefcase, leave it in the yard," Valenzuela said.

"Right. Leave the case in the yard. I won't forget."

Rashad looked over at Mati. "The kid'll go with you, keep you comp'ny."

Teddy turned, unslinging his Uzi and waving the stubby barrel. Mati got up, wiping his hands on his pants, and came toward them. It didn't seem to matter to him one way or the other.

They held back at the bend in the road, waiting, letting Mel and Mati continue on toward the opening in the stone fence.

"Might as well get everybody in the yard," Rashad said. "Do 'em all at one time."

"IT'S MATI," Tali said, surprised. "And Mr. Bandy?"

Davis watched them come through the gate and start up the drive, Mel carrying his expensive alligator case. The light blue lawyer and the skinny Yemenite in his fake leather jacket. They didn't go together, wouldn't have anything to say to each other. They had both been pushed into this, brought here—the sound of the car last night, the headlights reflecting in the darkness.

"Did they come here by themselves?" Tali was still speculating. There was no sign of the three gunmen.

But Davis wasn't going to get into a conversation about it. He said, "Take the shotgun. Watch the car and see if anybody tries to circle around the other side. If they do, shoot them. Don't tell me about it, shoot them."

Picking up the shotgun, she looked over at him. His tone was quiet, but he was concentrating now, not wasting words, raising the Mauser and extending the barrel out the window.

"They don't want to come out," Davis said. "They send Mel . . . no, there they are." He brought the Mauser to his shoulder but waited. They were beyond the stone fence, near the gate and the section that had been blown apart. He could see little more of them than heads and shoulders and realized that the ground sloped away toward the wadi.

"I see them," Tali said.

He told her to concentrate on the one nearest the gate opening, the one with the long hair and a scarf or bandana covering his head. Mel and Mati, who was dragging behind, were coming over from the drive now, crossing the grass toward the middle of the yard.

Mel moved carefully, his gaze holding on the front

windows. Mati's hands were in his pockets. He seemed to have no purpose other than to watch what was going on.

"Sergeant, you in there?"

"Right here," Davis said.

"I can't see you. . . . Where's Rosen?"

"You want to come in?"

"No, I'm supposed to stay here. Is that Rosen—hey, Rosie, is that you?"

"He's in the can," Davis said.

Mel thought that was funny. "Listen, you mind if I use it after? I've got kind of a nervous bladder. I don't know what the fuck I'm doing here at all." He glanced over his shoulder, then looked back at the windows. "I'm sure you understand this isn't my idea. I'm supposed to be on a plane in half an hour."

"You're not coming in," Davis said, "what do you want?"

"I'm speaking for them, you understand. None of this is my idea."

Davis waited.

"They want to offer you something. A hundred thousand dollars."

The three gunmen were at the stone fence now, not more than a few yards separating them. He would have to squeeze and fire and snap the next two shots, though he would be sure of getting the first one. Davis placed the front sight on Valenzuela, then raised his head to look at Mel again.

"You hear what I said? A hundred thousand. It's in here." Mel raised the attaché case.

"For what?"

"If you leave. Get out of here."

"Alone?"

"You can take the girl."

"But leave Rosen, huh? Just a minute." Davis turned to look at Tali. She was staring at him and seemed more tense than a few moments before.

"They don't know," Davis said to her.

"But if he's already dead? They'll come in to see him, won't they?"

Davis looked out at Mel.

"Rosen says he doesn't like the idea."

"Jesus—" Mel was shaking his head. "Look, tell him I'm sorry, but there's nothing I can do about this. You can stay here and see what happens or you can accept the hundred grand and leave. That's it."

"Mr. Rosen's money, huh?"

"What difference does it make?" Mel said. "You want to see it?" He went down to one knee, placed the attaché case on the grass, snapped it open, and turned the lid toward him to show Davis the open case. "Can you see it? That's a hundred grand, man."

"Where's the rest?" Davis said.

"What rest?"

"We started with two hundred thousand," Davis said. "You sent him five. Where's the rest?"

"Well, see, what they're doing, they're splitting it with you, giving you the bigger half. What do you say?"

Davis was silent. He watched some of the hundred-dollar bills blow out of the case as a wind stirred in from the desert. Mel said, "Jesus Christ—" and almost fell making a grab for them.

"All right? Come on, before it blows away."

Davis waited. He said then, "Tell them, they want to give me the whole thing, it's a deal."

"Christ, this is a hundred grand here!" Mel said. "What do you want?"

"I just told you, I want it all," Davis said. "Or I stay here and they sit out in the sun till the police or an Israeli Army patrol comes along."

"I'll have to ask them," Mel said. He rose, turning, as more bills blew out of the briefcase, and yelled toward the fence, "He says he wants the whole thing!" Mel waited. "What?"

Davis held the sight on Valenzuela. He watched him wave for Mel to come back.

Mel turned to the windows again. "I guess they want to talk it over." Mel stooped to close the briefcase, but Valenzuela called something to him and Mel straightened and walked off, glancing back at the money blowing, swirling across the yard, then motioned to Mati to come with him.

"Watch them," Davis said.

Tali glanced at him, saw him move to Mr. Rosen's body and pull back the blanket. She looked out the window and then at the Marine again. He was lifting Mr. Rosen's hands now—the bent arms rising stiffly with the hands—then drawing the Colt automatic from its holster and placing it on the compress bandage covering Mr. Rosen's wound, making sure the safety was off. It shocked her and made no sense.

"Why are you doing that?"

"Watch outside."

Davis took another compress from the pack of bandages on the floor, placed it over the automatic, and brought Rosen's hands down to cover the compress. The grip of the Colt, part of it, was all that showed.

"Please, what are you *do*ing?"

Davis glanced out the window, seeing the five of them at the opening in the fence. He picked up Dr. Morris' heavy Enfield revolver from the floor and tried it in the shoulder holster. It rested too high beneath his left arm. He pulled the gun out and stuck it into the waist of his trousers.

He said to Tali then, "I've thought of what I want to tell them."

"SAY, FINE, he can have the whole thing," Rashad said. "What's the difference?"

"Watch them," Valenzuela said to Teddy. He motioned Rashad away from Mel and the Arab-looking kid and they moved down the road toward the gray car.

"He won't believe it," Valenzuela said. "We're agreeing too quick. Why would we do it?"

"You want to sit here," Rashad said, "wait till tomorrow to make it look real? What's the difference? A hundred, a hundred ninety-five, if he smells something he'll smell it either way. No, I believe what he's doing, he's putting it all on one roll. Got nothing to lose. He knows we're playing with the man's money. He sees a chance to take it all. But tell me, how's he gonna get out with it? Man, we're standing there."

"He's pulling something," Valenzuela said.

"Pulling what? He hasn't had time to think about it. He's seeing how much he can get, that's all. He's got nothing to lose, we got nothing to lose giving it to him."

"Mel said there's no sign of Rosen."

"I agree with Teddy, the man's probably been hit," Rashad said. "But he's in there, isn't he? No place else he could be."

Valenzuela thought about it a little more. Finally he said, "All right. We'll say we'll give him the whole thing. The other half when he comes out."

MEL RETURNED to the middle of the yard, Mati trailing.

"Sergeant!"

He stopped, looking around, and began picking up the bills that were scattered about the grass.

Davis waited, watching from the window. He saw Mati pick up several of the bills and slip one in his pocket as he walked over to the lawyer with the rest. Davis glanced at Tali. He was very tense now and it was a moment of relief.

"You see that?"

"Mati takes care of himself," Tali said. "I hope nothing happens to him."

The lawyer was squinting, looking this way again.

"Sergeant? . . . They said okay. You can have the whole thing."

Just like that, Davis thought. They give away money.

"They said, you come out, get the briefcase here. One of them will come over and give you the rest."

"Tell them I want to see all three of them," Davis said. "If I come out, I don't want anybody staying back there behind the wall. All three of them have to come out."

Mel shrugged. It didn't make any difference to him. He looked at Mati and said something and Mati started back toward the fence. They had given Mati something to do.

"You understand? All three of them," Davis said.

Mel was nodding. "He'll tell them."

"They give me the money and I'll give them Rosen." Davis waited, making sure the lawyer heard him. "I'll even bring him out."

Mel was alert again, studying the windows. "You mean when you leave, they won't have to go in and get him?"

"I said I'll bring him out."

"Well—what does he have to say about that?"

"Nothing," Davis said.

Mel hesitated. "I don't quite understand."

"You don't have to. Go tell them."

"Just a minute," Mel said. He hurried back toward the stone fence.

Davis looked over at Tali. "You ready?"

The girl nodded, holding on tight to the shotgun resting on the window ledge.

"There are some other ways," Davis said, "but none that I like. Is it all right with you?"

The girl nodded again, afraid to speak.

"Then let's do it," Davis said.

He lowered the Mauser, resting it against the windowsill next to the girl, and walked over to where Rosen's body lay on the floor.

THEY CAME with the lawyer and Mati walking in front of them: Valenzuela and Teddy carrying the submachine guns at their sides; Rashad in the middle with a canvas athletic bag. The rest of the money would be in the bag, if Davis wanted to see it.

And a gun, Davis thought, watching them. He was holding Rosen in his arms, the body bent enough to appear natural from a distance, the head stiffly erect against Davis' shoulder. He tried not to look at Rosen's face. He stepped over the couch blocking the doorway and crossed the patio to the yard.

They saw him now. They were looking at him, the five of them coming across the grass from the fence, Davis approaching them from the desert house to meet where the money was. The five men arrived first. Mati walked aside. The lawyer was more subtle. He began picking up hundred-dollar bills as he moved away from them.

Valenzuela, at about thirty feet, said, "What's the matter with him?"

Davis didn't answer. He approached to within ten feet, almost to the open briefcase, before sinking to one knee and lowering Rosen's body to the ground. He remained there, looking up at them. He wished the two with the machine guns were standing together and not separated by Rashad. Their clothes were dusty and stained with sweat marks. They were dark figures with the sun behind them. The sun was all right, it didn't bother him. It outlined them cleanly. They had not taken their eyes off Rosen. Davis remained on one knee, his left hand resting on Rosen's hands.

"Well," Rashad said, "here we are." He was holding the canvas bag in front of him now, his hand inside the opening. Looking at Rosen's face, the closed eyes, he said, "What'd you bother for?"

In the moment before it happened, Davis could see it happening.

He said, "We bring out our dead."

He lifted Rosen's hands, drew the Colt .38 from beneath the compress bandage, and shot Rashad in the chest as the man's hand was coming out of the bag. Davis saw him punched sideways, but couldn't wait to see if he was going down.

He shot Valenzuela in the stomach and in the chest as the Uzi was pointing at him, the Uzi going up in the air as Valenzuela was socked hard and Davis knew he was out of it.

Somebody was yelling something, the one with the scarf tied over his hair like a pirate.

He shot Teddy in the face as Teddy was crouching to fire and saw his arms go up with the Uzi, his chest exposed, and shot him again, in the chest.

He had to get to Rashad because he wasn't sure of

Rashad, and by the time he put the Colt on him, shit, he was a moment too late, the Colt pointing at a Beretta. The Beretta fired first and Davis felt it this time—not like the time getting in the Medevac with the blood pouring out of his leg—he felt the bullet tear into his thigh, the same leg, three times now, leg wounds, three times and out of it, home, as he held the Colt on Rashad with Rashad looking at it and shot him four times in the chest. There. One round left in the Colt and he didn't need Dr. Morris' revolver stuck in his pants. It was uncomfortable. He pulled it out and dropped it on the ground. He was aware of the silence. He looked at Valenzuela and the other one, knowing they were dead, and shoved the Colt into the shoulder holster and tried to stand up, then had to try again before he made it. His leg didn't hurt yet, it was a reaction, seeing the blood and afraid to touch the leg, afraid it might shatter if he stood on it; but he was all right now, he was up. He was sweating a lot.

Mati came over to him first and tried to help him, offering to hold him up; but he was okay he told Mati. He heard Mel's voice and heard Tali. She was saying, "David . . ." coming out to them. It always surprised him when he heard her say his name.

Mel was picking up the rest of the loose bills, putting them in the briefcase. He took the canvas bag from Rashad, trying to do it without touching him.

Mel said, "Wow," reverently, then said it a few more times. "I don't believe it. Christ, I was standing right there—you know how long that took? About eight seconds, no more than ten." He walked over toward Davis, looking down at Rosen. "I'm very sorry about Rosie, but—well, what can you say, uh?" Now he was looking at Davis.

"Are you all right?"

"I will be."

Davis looked at Tali and smiled at her worried expression. He was stooped slightly, holding his thigh, pressing his hand against it. In a minute he'd go in the house and take a look and get it cleaned up. The bullet was still in his leg and he'd have to go to the hospital in Eilat, but it didn't hurt at all right now. He'd worry about the hospital later.

"When I say the company is gonna be most grateful to you, that's an understatement," Mel said. "And I know they won't question my giving you this. In fact, we spoke before about getting these funds back home, which we can discuss again later on. Sergeant, with my deepest gratitude." He extended a pack of hundred-dollar bills to Davis.

"What's that?"

"Ten thousand dollars," Mel said. "You earned it."

Davis said, "All this, it's the money that was sent to Rosen, right?"

Tali stepped in. "You brought it to the hotel yourself. You saw it."

He said to Mel, "So it isn't company money anymore, is it?"

"Well, insofar as it's recovered money," Mel said.

"Recovered from what?" Davis said. "They took Rosen's money from you and gave it to me. What I want to know is, how come you're offering me some of my own money?"

"Now wait a minute," Mel said. "All we're really talking about is a reward. And I mean ten big ones, not a few bucks."

Davis reached over and took the briefcase from him, brought his hand up bloody from the wound, and took the canvas bag.

"I don't think I need a reward," Davis said. "Why don't I just settle for what's mine?"

Mel wasn't sure if he was serious and tried to smile. He said, "Hey, come on. You can't just walk off with a hundred and ninety-five thousand dollars, for Christ sake."

"Why not?" Davis said.

It seemed that simple. Why not?